ESMERALDA

Also by the Author

ROSS'S GAP
ANTELOPE SPRINGS

ESMERALDA

G. Clifton Wisler

Walker and Company
New York

All the characters and events portrayed in this story are fictitious.

First published in the United States of America in 1989
by Walker Publishing Company, Inc.

Published simultaneously in Canada by Thomas Allen & Son Canada, Limited, Markham, Ontario.

Library of Congress Cataloging-in-Publication Data

Wisler, G. Clifton.
Esmeralda / G. Clifton Wisler.
p. cm.
ISBN 0-8027-4092-8
I. Title.
PS3573.I877E86 1989
813'.54—dc 19 88-30850
CIP

Printed in the United States of America

10 9 8 7 6 5 4 3 2 1

Remembering
Lucille McCormick Wisler
lover of books

ESMERALDA

CHAPTER 1

WESTERN Kansas awoke to a shower of golden sunlight that bright March morning. Winter had finally given way to the crisp touch of spring, and wildflowers shook themselves free of dewdrops in the calm dawn breeze that stirred the tall grasslands along the Arkansas River. In the distance a thin black plume told of the approach of the westbound freight due in at nearby Honey Springs Station. Gradually the faint chugging sounds of the locomotive mixed with the grinding and whining of brakes as the train grew near.

There was nothing unusual about the scene. By 1883 even the prairie dogs and field mice had grown accustomed to the shiny rails of the Atchison, Topeka, and Santa Fe Railroad. The trains that came and went ushered in commerce and prosperity. They carried Colorado gold and Texas cattle eastward and brought hearty settlers, farm tools, and eastern dreamers to the West. They attracted another breed, too.

"That's the train with the payroll sacks pullin' in now," George Stapleton explained as he handed his spyglass to his elder brother Frank.

"Right on time, too," Frank observed. "Not like that one over at Wells City. Don't them railroad folks know it makes it hard on us when they don't keep to their schedules?"

"Write 'em a letter, why don't you, Frank?" Tom, the youngest brother, suggested. "Or get Hollie to do it. He knows how to sweeten up words so them gals melt right in his hands. That right, Hollie?"

Holland Sisk grinned and nodded his head. Well, maybe they didn't melt exactly, but their eyes always seemed to invite his attentions, didn't they? And if it wasn't for Holland being on such good terms with the daughter of the dispatcher over in Hutchinson, the Stapletons would still be raiding dispatch riders and mercantile stores.

"What is it the gals see in you anyway, Hollie?" George asked.

"Must be my smile," Holland said, polishing his teeth with a bit of cedar bark. "Or my curly hair. Or my manly physique."

Holland stretched to his full five feet ten inches and tried to straighten the left leg that had been hamstrung three long years before. His long blond locks were neatly combed back from his forehead, and a mustache followed the contour of his upper lip, making him appear older than his seventeen years.

"More likely your imagination," Tom said, laughing.

Frank flashed a stern scowl, and the others grew quiet.

"Don't forget the purpose at hand," the eldest Stapleton warned. "We've got business to tend."

"Now?" George asked, taking the spyglass and examining the stationhouse.

"Give 'em leave to unload that payroll and get along out o' there," Frank replied. "For our purpose, it's best there ain't too many of 'em about."

"Don't you want an audience, big brother?" Tom asked.

"No, I've got no love o' dramatics, Tom. You always like to watch those little operettas in Dodge, I know, but I wouldn't want to be remembered all that well. And there's always the odd chance one o' those folks might have a pistol packed away."

"Leave that to me," Newton Shanklin grumbled.

The dark-eyed Shanklin fondled a silver-plated Remington revolver and grinned cruelly. Barrel-chested and a bit stumpy, Shanklin looked more the part of a Kansas farmer than a cold-blooded killer. Nevertheless, the Remington had concluded more than one argument in the most final of means, and Newt Shanklin was a name known to frighten schoolboys on dark, stormy eves.

"Train's pullin' out," George said, and the others instantly tensed.

"Where's that boy gotten to with the horses?" Shanklin complained. "Fool stableboy's never . . . "

"He's waterin' the mounts," Holland explained. "Don't you worry about Cle. He'll be along with the horses when it's time."

"Best we wait and make sure," George declared. "Know you boys go back a ways, Hollie, and young Smith's been steady enough when it's been called for, but you got to admit he gets carried away where the stock's concerned."

"Boy's a dreamer," Shanklin growled. "Near wandered right into that posse south o' Cottonwood Falls."

"They'd never mistook him for a member of the Stapleton gang," Holland argued. "And poor Cle'd never tell 'em anything even if they threw a rope 'round his neck."

"He does his job," Frank said, ending the discussion. "Here he comes now."

The sixth and last member of the Stapleton band was Cleophus Smith. Wiry-haired, seventeen, and a hair short of five and a half feet tall, the boy possessed the iron grip and stout shoulders of the blacksmith his Uncle Abner had been teaching him to be when the Stapletons had fled into town, horseless and bare moments ahead of a posse. Young Cle had provided remounts at his uncle's expense.

"Now, you got to take me along," the boy had insisted. The Stapletons had been hard-pressed and chose not to argue. For two years now Cle had tended the horses and kept them healthy. When it came time to visit a rail depot or freight office, Cle Smith had been there to hold the horses ready and lead the flight.

Perhaps more important, Cle had introduced Frank Stapleton to young Holland Sisk. Thereafter, prosperity and fame had followed.

"They ready, Cle?" Frank asked as Sisk led the horses toward the concealed outlaws.

"Watered and rested," Cle answered. "Ready for a hard run if it's needed."

"Hope it isn't," George said, turning toward the silent station. "I ain't seen a soul come or go. With luck, the place'll be empty."

"Give me leave to have a look," Holland announced. "I'll give the same signal as always, all right?"

"Go, son," Frank declared. "See you're to the right if trouble breaks out. We'll open up on the room goin' left to right."

"Sure," Shanklin grumbled. "Let's get to it."

"Yeah," Tom agreed. "Sun's risin' fast now."

Frank waved Holland toward the station and followed somewhat more slowly with the others.

Cle Smith brought the horses along last of all. It vexed him sometimes, being left out of the high drama, the real excitement. Then, too, he worried Holland might encounter some trial that smooth talk and an easy smile couldn't handle. The rest of his life Holland would limp because he'd dallied with the wife of a Cimarron muleskinner. That muleskinner had done a fine job on Hollie's hamstring, though it was generally agreed the knife had been intended for the boy's vitals.

"Fourteen and chasin' married ladies," Cle muttered, grinning. It had always been a source of pride and amazement that Holland Sisk, who could have listed a thousand friends if he chose to make the effort, should have befriended Cleophus Smith. Cleophus! Oh, how the boys and girls at school had tormented him because of that name! Cleophus, runt of the family and plain-faced to boot! A lifetime as the butt of every schoolboy prank and town jest had turned Cle Smith's hide leathery tough and his heart near as hard.

He was well-suited to his present work. Not dashing or quick with a gun, granted, but Cle was utterly and totally fearless. Life, he often told himself, had been one unceasing hour of pain followed by another, and so there need be no dread of its conclusion.

At twelve he'd been consigned by his father to shovel dung in his uncle's stable. By fourteen he'd developed a blacksmith's build and a fiery temper that punished the mildest taunt severely. At fifteen he'd outfitted the Stapletons and become the youngest member of their band.

A hundred yards away, in the stationhouse, the other young member of the gang leaned on a countertop and stared at the train schedule written in chalk on a large black slate.

"Help you, son?" asked a smallish clerk with thinning silvery hair.

"You got a train headed along to Dodge City 'fore noon?" Holland asked.

"No eastbound passenger trains due till tomorrow, son," the clerk answered. "Might try to jump the six o'clock freight. Doesn't stop here, mind you. Tomorrow's the first regular run."

"Just my luck!" Holland complained in mock anger. He limped along to an empty table on the far left side of the small hall that doubled as waiting room and café. Just behind him two ladies sipped coffee and nervously glanced at a clock. Either a train was late or someone had failed to show up to bring them home. On the far wall, beside the door, sat a dozing teamster. Beside him rested a bullwhip, and a small valise was wedged beneath his chair.

"Got business in Dodge, do you?" one of the women asked.

"Yes'm," Holland answered, grinning. "You?"

"Oh, dear me, no," the woman replied. "My sister Glory and I are waiting for our brother. We're home on school holiday."

"Oh?" Holland asked, momentarily distracted from the twin money bags he'd already spied beneath the freight counter.

"Do you go to school, Mr.—"

"Shields," Holland said. "Homer Shields. No, ma'am, I fear I never took to numbers and letters. I'm a fair carpenter, though."

"Carpenter?" the clerk asked. "With hands like yours? More likely card handler or piano jockey."

Holland stared angrily at the clerk, then pulled out a cigar from his coat pocket and stepped to the door.

"Interrupt your game, did I, sonny?" the clerk called.

Holland glared at the fool, then struck a match, lit the cigar, and puffed hard until the tip glowed brightly. He then blew three successive circles of smoke before returning to the far lefthand table.

"Sir, please, I can't abide tobacco," the prettier of the young women cried.

"I wouldn't offend you for the world, ma'am," Holland said, gallantly crushing the cigar beneath his boot.

Tom Stapleton sauntered inside the room then, followed by his brothers.

"When's the westbound due?" Frank asked.

"Late this afternoon," the clerk said, pointing to the slate. "Can I sell you boys tickets?"

"No, we won't be travelin' by rail," Frank replied. "Got horses waitin'."

"Then why . . ."

George Stapleton drew a Colt revolver from his hip and tapped its barrel on the counter. The ladies shrank back in terror, and Holland flashed a small Colt revolver and took possession of their pocketbooks. The teamster awoke and made a grab for his whip. Tom Stapleton kicked it away, then clubbed the man across the back of the head with a pistol barrel.

"Frank, look out!" Holland cried as the clerk reached beneath the counter.

Quick as lightning, Newt Shanklin fired a bullet through the clerk's nose. The stricken railroader froze a second, then collapsed to the floor.

"All right," Frank said, hopping over the counter and grabbing the payroll bags. "Let's get after it."

Tom and George Stapleton tore open the money bags and inspected the contents. Frank, meanwhile, rifled the office, locating a few letters containing banknotes and a box or two with useful goods within. Shanklin pried open the teamster's valise and tore two hundred dollars in greenbacks from the lining. Holland found thirty dollars in the handbags. He also took a gold watch, then kissed both ladies before departing.

"You scoundrel!" one of the women screamed. "My brother will see you hanged for this outrage. That was my mother's watch."

"Well, you thank her for it," Holland answered, tipping his hat. "Nice meetin' you, ma'am."

The second woman actually waved, and the outlaws laughed heartily.

"Hey, would you look at this here?" Frank bellowed as he tore apart the clerk's desk. "New poster. Fine likenesses this time, Newt."

"Let me see," the killer said, snatching the poster and staring at the crude drawing of a sneering, black-haired gunman. "Better'n the last, I'd agree. 'Specially o' Tom."

The younger Stapleton agreed, bowing slightly as if the comment warranted some recognition.

"Well, look there, though!" George barked. "Misspelled our name."

True enough, the poster read "Staleton gang." And it failed entirely to mention Sisk or Smith.

"I'll help 'em remember," Frank promised, taking an ax from the storeroom and splintering the counter. Then he erased the train schedules from the slate and wrote "Stapletons."

"Don't know it's wise to advertise who was here, Frank," George argued.

"Doesn't matter," Frank replied. "Those gals'll chirp like songbirds. 'Bout time this railroad takes notice, too. A mere five-hundred-dollar reward, and that only if we're convicted. Lord, I hear Turkey Tom Hunter's head goes at five thousand, and he only killed one fool senator."

"Wrong senator, I expect," Shanklin noted. "Now, let's finish up and ride. I don't care much for hangin' around once the business is concluded."

"He's right," George declared.

"Sure," Frank agreed.

And so the money was packed in a flour sack, and Frank led his companions over to where Cle and Holland waited with the horses.

"Fair take, eh?" Cle asked.

"I figure ten thousand in the money sacks," Tom explained. "More loose."

"Ten thousand?" Cle asked, whooping. "Lord, there's not that much money in all Kansas, is there?"

"Is now," Frank said, tying the sack to his saddle horn. "And we got it."

The others hollered their approval, and Frank led the way westward, down into the river so that the streambed would conceal their tracks. Later they would emerge in the first of a series of gullies. A half day's ride through rough country would lead to Ma Totley's Amusement Palace, where comforts could be procured at a price. The Stapletons had the price often and were frequent guests.

"Westward ho," Frank called, grinning. His companions all knew the meaning of those words. Memories of perfumed pillows and piano music flowed between their ears, and even Cle Smith managed a rare grin.

"Hey, Tom, did you tear down the telegraph wire?" Frank asked as they splashed into the river.

"Lord, didn't George?" the youngest brother asked.

"Fool of a brother," George growled. "That was your job. Can't you do anything right?"

"I thought . . . "

Frank yelled for silence, then drew out a long-barreled

Winchester. After steadying the rifle, he fired. A hundred yards away the telegraph wire snapped and dangled helplessly from its wooden pole.

"Fine shot, that," Shanklin observed. "Best hope they didn't get word out first."

"Figure that teamster for a dot an' dash man?" George asked, laughing. "Or maybe one o' the ladies?"

"Maybe the clerk came back to life," Holland suggested.

"Not a prayer for that one," Shanklin barked. "What I shoot stays dead."

Yes, Holland Sisk thought as he nodded his head. That was certainly true enough.

The Stapleton gang rode a mile and a quarter through the sandy bottom of the Arkansas before emerging into a narrow ravine. Frank then led the way through the flat farmland and rounded hills south of the river to an abandoned dugout once frequented by buffalo hunters.

"Thought we'd make for Ma Totley's," Tom complained.

"Not today," Frank explained. "Got to split the take first. Then we ought to let our trail cool a bit."

"Frank, ain't nobody followin' us, not for a day at best," Shanklin argued.

"So it'd seem," Frank admitted. "But I got a strange feelin' comin' over me, and I think we're holin' up till dark right here. Put the horses in yon shed, Cle. Tom, you and Hollie see 'bout collectin' us some stove wood. George, you figure we can slice some o' that ham and fry up some beans?"

"I'd say so," George responded.

"Then let's set to it. I've got a hunger."

If there were trackers searching the plain for the Stapletons, they must surely have been shadows, for no soul appeared within view of the dugout all that day nor the following night. The outlaws kept a careful watch, four hours on and four off. Still, no hint of danger emerged.

"Ever wish you'd taken a different road?" Cle asked Holland when the two of them took over the midnight watch.

"What road?" Holland asked. "I never came to any fork of trails, Cle. I just put one foot ahead o' t'other and did my best to stay alive. It's all an orphan can do."

"Guess so. Still, I wish just once I could ride into town with my head held high and tell 'em all I ride with Frank Stapleton."

"Sure way to get yourself killed."

"Sure, and I'll never do it. I would like to tell some o' them, though."

"You wouldn't want your ma to know, though. She set great store by the Bible, as I recall."

"She's dead, and Pa might's well be. He gave me a spade and bid me good-bye. I crossed him from my mind thereafter."

"You've got brothers and sisters, though."

"I got myself. And only a couple o' friends worth mentionin'."

"Yeah, I know," Holland muttered. "I sometimes wish I'd stayed around town, maybe taken to farmwork like ole man Kraft said I should. But once I got lamed, there wasn't much choice. A one-legged man has his choices reduced considerable."

"Maybe you'll find yourself a rich widow, tickle her fancy. She'll take care o' you, all right, Hollie."

"With my share o' ten thousand, I might just buy out Ma Totley, go into the amusements business."

"No, you'd wear out all the merchandise your own self," Cle said, laughing. "It's a thought, though, ain't it? My share'd be considerable. Imagine that! A thousand dollars. I could buy that stable and hire Uncle Abner to do the shovelin'. Maybe we could go partners in a little mercantile off in Colorado. Lots o' new towns poppin' up in Ute country, so I hear."

"Maybe," Holland said, sighing. "Once we tire o' the game at hand. Or we get run a bit."

"Yeah, we're havin' our own way for now, ain't we?"

"Are indeed, Cle."

CHAPTER 2

THE success of the Stapleton gang did not escape the notice of the Atchison, Topeka, and Santa Fe management. New posters were printed, rewards were raised, and bands of armed riders swept both banks of the Arkansas—all to no avail. Still the brothers plagued the scattered stations of the railroad, appearing and vanishing as if by some bit of sorcery.

No one felt the Stapletons' sting more than Garner McFarlane, the security director for the railroad's western district. From his suite in the Kansas Hotel in far-off Topeka, he read each dispatch and drank in each report of fresh outrage with growing resolve. And finally he phrased a wire.

HAVE COMMISSION, it read in part. *PARTICULARS AWAIT YOUR ARRIVAL. WILL DEPOSIT RETAINER YOUR NAME BANK OF KANSAS. MCFARLANE.*

McFarlane then rang a desk bell, and his private secretary, a sour-faced young man named Brooks, entered the room.

"Send this," McFarlane instructed, handing over the cable. "And transfer a thousand dollars to Mr. Reid's account."

Brooks raised an eyebrow, nodded to himself, and set off on his duties.

It was three days before the telegram brought a response. Then a smallish figure strode into the outer office manned by Brooks, handed the secretary a finely engraved business card, and took a seat in the far corner, facing both doors.

"Mr. Copley Reid, Washington," Brooks read aloud. "I'll inform Mr. McFarlane at once," Brooks said, stepping away from his desk and entering the larger room used by McFarlane.

Reid wasn't the least surprised when McFarlane appeared in person to welcome him a moment later.

"Come in, Reid," the security director urged, waving the newcomer through the door. "I trust you had a pleasant trip."

"Long and dusty," Reid grumbled.

"I'll see you're put in the President's Suite," McFarlane responded. Topeka, being a railroad town, reserved its best accommodations not for the chief executive of the republic but for the proprietor of the Atchison, Topeka, and Santa Fe Railroad.

Reid nodded. The slightest trace of a grin crossed his emotionless lips. Pale and thin, with brass wire-rimmed spectacles set atop a pointed nose, Copley Reid seemed ill at ease. His small, delicate fingers examined the rich fabric of McFarlane's sofa before taking a seat.

"Your card says Washington," McFarlane noted. "Have you been in the capital of late?"

"You found me in Omaha, didn't you?" Reid asked in turn. "Truth is, it's been a time since I've held residence anywhere. I had those cards printed a lifetime ago. They suit me well enough. The important thing is you know it's me, not some prairie halfwit out to make money at my expense."

"Oh, there's no mistaking you, Reid. You may recall we met when I worked for the Union Pacific up in the Medicine Bow country. You were sketching the work camps at the time."

"Yes," Reid said, recalling.

"You captured the whole westward movement in that painting on the wall behind me you did of Rock Springs Station. Even the fancy girls hanging out their laundry."

Reid gazed a minute at the picture. It was, indeed, one of his better efforts, though a far cry from the masterpieces he had hoped to create when he first left Philadelphia for the Rockies. That masterpiece was as elusive as a rainbow trout, and he'd never quite accomplished what he'd hoped.

Now he'd turned to another line.

"You remember that bit of business you did for us last November?" McFarlane asked when he saw his visitor had lost interest in the painting.

"Bit of business?" Reid asked, scratching his ear. "You mean Noley Barnes."

"Exactly. Well, it appears we have a worse problem now."

"The Stapletons," Reid offered. "Fine bunch, those fellows. I hear last week they passed a night at a schoolhouse over in Kingman. Noticed the place was low on books and slates, so they left the schoolmarm a thousand dollars to buy what she needed. Kidnapped a doctor from Dodge and took him all the way to Russell to treat a little girl's fever. You know the Hutchinson newspaper calls them Robin Hoods."

"I know all too well," McFarlane said, frowning heavily. "We send agents after them, and you'd think our men were the ones wanted for murder. Some of them are shot at, even killed. Three have just up and disappeared."

"The Stapletons are clever."

"They're thieves and murderers. Last week at Honey Springs they shot our clerk dead, cleared out the office, and robbed a pair of schoolgirls of their dead mama's watch. But by the time the papers finished, you'd have thought we were burning children in the back room!"

"How much did they get?"

"A ten-thousand-dollar payroll."

"And they struck you again the same week? Any men with half a mind would leave the country for a bit, spend some of that cash down Mexico way or in San Francisco. Any pattern to their raids? They pick on any one place or kind of shipment?"

"Not that I can see," McFarlane said, sighing. "They've hit mining supplies, ranch payrolls, cattle buyers, you name it."

"All in your district?"

"Mostly," McFarlanc grumbled. "They had the gall to hit the Chicago Flyer in Kansas City, though. They're afraid of nothing."

"Well, they've made at least one mistake then," Reid declared. "They should be afraid of me."

"They don't even know you, Reid. They've been chased by sheriffs, U.S. marshals, even a troop of cavalry."

"Too many men," Reid muttered. "No, you've got two problems really, and a posse won't solve either."

"Two problems? There are six of them by my reckoning."

"One man or six, it's all the same. Once you track them, they're just so many targets. Your problem is tracing their information source."

"What?"

"Isn't luck lets them nab a ten-thousand-dollar payroll. You've got somebody feeding them schedules, or else talking too much. Who's your dispatcher?"

"Rostin, in Hutchinson."

"Fire him, but first keep feeding him routes and such, only have another man do the real routing. We'll run a special train for those Stapleton boys."

"That's a tall order, Reid. I'm not sure the company will go for . . . "

"You want them caught, you'll do it. Now, there's another matter."

"Yes?"

"You'll need to counter this Robin Hood nonsense. So long as the people hide and supply these thieves, you've got no hope of catching them. Route your special train somewhere a lot of people are bound to witness the raid."

"There's a schoolhouse right alongside the station at Banwell Junction."

"Set it up. Now, you're offering a thousand apiece for the Stapletons, I understand."

"That's right. Dead or alive."

"I want two thousand for Frank and George, three for Newt Franklin. A thousand's fine for Tom and the hanger's-on."

"What?"

"Plus a quarter of the money I retrieve."

"Ten percent is the going rate! I can find a dozen men who would jump at such terms."

"I suggest you hire them then," Reid said, rising.

"Now hold on a minute, Reid. I've already sent you earnest money, and I'm willing to pay reasonable expenses."

"I don't discuss terms," Reid explained. "Meet my price or leave it. It's up to you."

"You're the very devil of a man to deal with."

"I can afford to be," Reid said, grinning. "I get results. Now, would you be drawing up an agreement?"

"Yes, yes," McFarlane complained. "I thank heaven for one thing, though."

"Oh?"

"At least you haven't taken the outlaw trail. The only reason those Stapletons haven't hurt us worse is that they've got little thinking behind them."

"They've got more than you imagine," Reid objected. "You got a line map?"

McFarlane rang his bell, then instructed Brooks to locate a survey map of the A, T, & SF. The secretary produced one as McFarlane completed writing out the agreement. The terms were as demanded, and there was little discussion before both men signed.

When Brooks brought the map, Reid spread it out on a nearby table, then instructed McFarlane to mark each robbery and record its date.

"I don't know that," McFarlane objected. "We'd have to wade through every report for the past year and a half."

"I'd suggest you get started then," Reid countered. "I can't read a man's mind without seeing how he operates."

"And just what will you be doing while we're readying your map?"

"Getting a bath," Reid explained. "This dust is wearing at me some."

Reid departed, and McFarlane peered at the map.

"Get the reports, Brooks," the security director mumbled. "Let's get started."

Copley Reid returned, freshly washed and cleanshaven, smelling a bit too much of lilacs but otherwise resembling a well-dressed gentleman of forty bound for an evening at the theatre. A pocket Colt was concealed by his vest, and a small dirk rested in the back of his right boot.

Anyone passing Reid in the street would judge him to be an eastern dandy, or perhaps a Chicagoan down to negotiate beef contracts with the railroad. No one would have suspected the truth.

"Ah, Mr. Reid," Brooks said when Reid reappeared at McFarlane's suite. "We've been quite busy with your project."

Mine? Reid wondered if the railroaders understood who was to benefit from the work.

"I'm near halfway finished," McFarlane explained when Reid approached the table. "Only the March reports left. You can see, they've been busy."

"Busy?" Reid cried, staring at the vast number of markings. "Sure there aren't but six of them? Mosby staged fewer attacks."

Reid then etched a mental picture of the railroad and the scattered towns linked together by its iron rails. He grinned as he read from one of the reports.

"Well, so that's it," Reid remarked.

"Notice something?" McFarlane asked. "What have you found?"

"Says here the Stapletons hit the place just after the freight pulled out. Good plan. Not many folks around to get in the way."

"I knew that all along," McFarlane complained. "Tell me something new."

"They always hit the outbound trains, usually at their second or third stop. Early, too."

"That's not much of a pattern."

"Sure, it is. We'll send our train in early as well. Now, there's a curious thing," Reid said, studying the map, then pulling out a report. He read rapidly, then scowled.

"Find something?" McFarlane asked.

"You won't like it much. Once or twice wouldn't make me sure, but here's five times straight where you've changed a run less than a day ahead of time. Even so, the Stapletons've known about it. Your dispatcher or somebody in his office is giving out the schedules, plain and simple."

"We'll solve that by following your plan."

"Sure. Be wise to keep a sharp eye on the man, not to mention his family and the other workers at the dispatch yard. If any of them like to talk, you have them watched."

"So, what do you think?"

"Tell you what I believe. I believe these fellows are either the luckiest folks ever born, or they've got better information about your railroad than you do yourself. They've got good timing, too. They hit quick, then get clear."

"So how will you go about putting an end to the raids?"

"By shooting them dead, I imagine."

"But how?"

"In my own way, McFarlane. And considering how word tends to get to the Stapletons so fast, I believe I'll keep my own counsel."

"Can't you tell me any part of it?"

"Figure it out on your own," Reid suggested. "You've got all the information."

Reid then stepped away, collected the maps, and headed out the office door. He didn't tarry long before climbing the stairs to his upper floor suite. The silk curtains and embroidered linens were scarcely noticed as he again spread out the maps and began tracing the movements of the Stapleton gang along the Arkansas. Once each month the gang seemed to pause. Immediately thereafter, it went on a rampage.

"Yes, you've got somebody feeding you schedules," Reid spoke to the map. "That won't keep your pockets filled anymore, though. Now you've crossed my trail, and your run's finished."

Secretly a part of him wished the Stapletons to take their ill-gotten cash and ride south, west, north, or wherever. But he knew there was a greed that tempted thieves to stretch their fingers out and grab for more. Always more. And in the end that greed was as good as a mousetrap for snaring them.

Copley Reid studied the map another hour, then marked out possible lairs and refuges. Several came to mind easily—bawdy houses that catered to trail hands, or taverns eager to trade a bottle of corn liquor to anyone for a few coins. Yes, the Stapletons and their cohorts were likely enjoying themselves in such a place that very moment. Reid imagined them each, the three brothers and Newton Shanklin in particular. The others, well, they were like as not boys run off an uncle's farm, eager to make their fortunes at the end of a pistol.

"Not much sport in such," Reid said as he bent over and opened a fancy brown leather case. Inside, the disassembled parts of his prize Alsweig Model 1880 rifle came into view. It took him but a few moments to screw each piece of stock or barrel in place and then to affix the delicate precision scope that allowed the rifle to find its target half a mile away.

Reid swung open the window and gazed through the sight at the citizens of Topeka calmly walking the street below. He adjusted the scope until he could stare at the shiny brass buttons of a cavalry lieutenant. He next fixed his sight on a banker's bulging middle.

Small boys played a game in the street, dodging horses and carts, taunting their elders with youthful cries.

"Where are you, Stapletons?" Reid whispered as he aimed the rifle again at the banker, then squeezed the trigger. If loaded, the high-caliber rifle would have torn the man's neat collar into shreds. As it was, the banker strolled on down the street in blissful ignorance.

"Sorry, Mr. Banker," Reid said, sighing as he rested the

rifle against the wall. "These bullets are reserved for others. You'll have to go on pushing papers and seizing farms, putting widows on the street and making paupers out of children."

It was, perhaps, an unfair indictment. It wasn't the Bank of Kansas that had sent Copley Reid from the house his grandfather had built in Hagerstown, Maryland. Another man had torn his father's heart in two and brought on his mother's premature death.

It would bring Reid the greatest pleasure to arrive at the bank next morning and withdraw a thousand dollars. More than once he'd watched a banker's pain-wracked face as fingers deftly counted off one banknote after another.

Wells Fargo would transport the funds eastward, all save a hundred dollars or so that would tide him over until the work commenced. Then Copley Reid would reap dollars like a Kansas farmer harvested corn, by peck and bushel.

Where would ten thousand dollars take him? Back to Austria, with its white winters and gracious architecture? To Bavaria or Holland? There were many places he might find distraction. But it wouldn't last long. The sport would beckon him back. The hunt would begin anew. And Reid would hasten to it like a starving man.

"And what about you, boys?" Reid whispered to the map. He envisioned George and Frank Stapleton sitting beside a flickering campfire. Perhaps brother Tom would hum a tune. Newt Shanklin would ready his pistols for fresh work, and the two youngsters, those mysterious, faceless young cohorts . . . what would they be about? One might tend the horses. The other might cook supper.

"How dark are your hearts, boys?" Reid inquired. They had a sense of humor, after all. Why else would they leave a thousand dollars with a schoolmarm? That story was legend. Less known was how the woman had departed on the first eastbound train, never to reappear. No books or slates arrived, either.

Was it the same with the Stapletons? Reid wondered. Was it greed that drove them, or the drama of the game? Did they desire more cash, or could they not stop their walk along the precipitous cliff? After all, a man who daily faced death could scarce help but feel more alive.

"Enjoy yourselves, boys," Reid said as he slowly rolled the map. "You've ridden far, but now it's about over."

He broke down the rifle and replaced its parts in their leather case. Then he prepared to spend a final night in the comfort of the large feather bed. Tomorrow Copley Reid would ride west, and the Stapletons would feel the sting of the Alsweig. Perhaps they would be sitting around the fire as the faint whine split the air. The first would fall with hardly a notice. The second, well, it would perhaps startle or confuse the survivors. The third and fourth, well, they would likely be caught on the run. As for all six, even Reid had his limits. He'd never hit that many targets from a single stand.

"Sleep well," Reid called out the window toward the distant plain. "Death's on its way."

CHAPTER 3

COPLEY Reid set out early the next morning. He paused only long enough to withdraw funds from the bank, dispatch most of the money at the Wells Fargo depot, and pick up a railroad pass and letters of introduction from Garner McFarlane. Then, equipped with a small valise and the leather case containing the Austrian rifle, Reid caught the westbound express headed toward Dodge City and beyond.

He got off the train at Honey Springs Station.

Little evidence of the Stapleton brothers' raid remained. A new clerk by the name of Hector Cash had taken charge of the place, and the ledgers were as neat and straight as the baggage counter.

"Don't know there's anybody can help you here," Cash told Reid. "I wasn't here myself, of course, and the Maxwell girls have gone back to their school. The old freighter, Barnaby Hobson, might still be around. He took a fair whack across his skull, so he won't recall much else. Still, he was here."

Reid nodded. He offered no other comment, and Cash grumbled that a "thank you" might be in order.

"McFarlane pays you a salary, doesn't he?" Reid responded. "It's your job to answer my questions, don't you think?"

Cash swallowed deeply, and Reid heard the clerk sigh with relief at his visitor's exit.

Hobson was easily found, since there wasn't much more to Honey Springs than the depot itself. On down the road a small church that doubled as a school stood alongside a mercantile and a small grog house. Hobson sat at the bar of the saloon, his bandaged head and rough clothes setting him apart from the pair of drifters who were the saloon's only other midday customers.

"Afternoon," Reid said as he sat on a barrel beside the freighter. "I'm called Reid."

"So?" Hobson replied.

"I understand the Stapleton boys helped themselves to some of your belongings. I'm hunting them."

"Huntin'?"

"That's right," Reid explained. "The railroad and the law don't seem able to bring them to justice."

"And you will?" Hobson asked, laughing. "There were five of 'em hit the depot, you know. Newt Shanklin himself'd peel you and swallow you whole, friend."

"Would he?" Reid asked, his eyes burning. "Trust me to know my business, Hobson. Now, what can you tell me about the way they did it?"

"Friend, you got gumption. That's for certain. All right, I'll tell you what I recall of it. My head's been fuzzy on most of it, but I do recall a youngster, a smilin' fellow with a limp, came in first. He did some conversin' 'bout schedules, then visited with a pair o' schoolgirls. Bit later he took out a cigar and lit it up. Walked to the door, puffed that cigar, and next thing I knew, the place was full o' Stapletons. Shanklin, too."

"This boy. Can you describe him?"

"Well," Hobson said, rubbing his hands together, "as I recall he had a mustache. Heavy one for a young fellow. Wasn't too tall, just a hair more'n you. And his right leg was bad, like a horse'd fell on it. He was a gimp for certain."

"Did the boy seem on good terms with the clerk?"

"To tell the truth, that one was slick as Colorado ice. He had an easy smile, and it seemed to me he could be the kind to find out what he wanted just by sittin' 'round and gabbin'. I couldn't say he knew the clerk, nor the girls neither, and he took their pocketbooks, you know. Even so, I think the one of 'em'd ridden off with him."

"They come early?"

"Just after dawn. I'd judge they waited for the train to come and go, then pounced."

"Anything else strike you strange?"

"Well, friend, I was clubbed senseless 'fore they got along with it much. Can't say much more'n I have already."

"Well, I'm grateful for that."

"How grateful? You know they pure cleaned me out. If you catch up with 'em, you'll have reward money comin'."

"True enough," Reid said, pulling a crisp ten-dollar banknote from his pocket and passing it along to Hobson. "Only fair to share the bounty, isn't it?"

"Only fair," Hobson agreed. "I think o' somethin' else, how do I get it to you?"

"Just drop it off at the nearest station, and tell them it's to go to Garner McFarlane. He'll see it gets to me."

"Fair enough. And listen. If you happen across that bunch, you see they get their due. My head's still ringin'."

"Oh, I'll find them," Reid assured his companion. "And they'll pay sure as the sun rises and falls."

By evening Copley Reid was in Dodge City. In the two days that followed he drifted from one station to another, questioning clerks and passengers who had suffered at the hands of the Stapleton gang. Moreover, Reid visited saloons and amusement houses. Around gaming tables and in back halls he learned more and more.

"Oh, Frank Stapleton loves this town," a good-natured barmaid in Newton explained. "Brings us a lot of business, you know. I know they say he's done some terrible things, but he's all sugar and silver when he's here."

In the isolated farming towns near Hutchinson, where the railroad had never been particularly popular, Reid found only hostile stares in answer to his inquiries.

"Whatever I know, I keep it to myself," one old-timer explained. "Most everybody hereabouts has gotten a bit of seed money from those Stapleton boys. What's the railroad ever done for anybody?"

Reid decided his appearance didn't much help. A harsh north wind had blown down out of the Dakota badlands, and he'd flung an old army greatcoat left from his campaigning days across his shoulders. That coat gave him a stunted, shadowy appearance, and he noticed come dusk the children seemed to give him lots of room on the street.

"Well, you look like the devil himself sometimes," Reid told himself. "And you've got no time to nod to kids anyway!"

At Burton, just east of Hutchinson, he checked into a small rooming house and wandered the streets. Down at the Riverside Saloon, he found himself watching a smiling young man wearing neatly creased trousers, a fine shirt with lace cuffs, and a new felt hat tilted arrogantly to one side.

"That boy appears familiar to me," Reid told a barmaid. "Know him?"

"Everybody knows Howard," she explained. "He's in here every so often, showing the girls card tricks, throwing dice, or playing blackjack. He's a charmer. Why, he's talked his way out of more trouble and into more company than about anybody I've ever seen."

"Seems a pleasant sort, I'll admit."

"Shame about his leg, though. Was tomahawked by wild Indians, to hear him tell it."

"Limps bad, does he?"

"Oh, not too bad," she said, growing nervous at Reid's heightened interest. "What'd you say your name was, mister?"

"Copley Reid."

"What business are you in?"

"Oh, no business," he said, laughing. "Guess you could call me a man of leisure."

"Oh?"

"I'm a painter," Reid explained, taking out a pencil and making a rough sketch of her face on a tally sheet. "See?"

"You're good," she said, joining him at the table. "Maybe later on you'd like to do me up proper."

"I would indeed, only I leave early for Topeka tomorrow morning. Maybe next time I'm here."

"I'll expect that, Mr. Reid."

His eyes followed her all the way to the bar before glancing back at young Howard. His smile faded when he discovered the boy gone.

Well, after all, it wouldn't do to alert the Stapletons. This boy wouldn't make much difference when it came right down to it. And if the turncoat dispatcher habited saloons, Reid judged that smiling Howard, or whatever his true name was, wouldn't have much difficulty learning anything he wished.

Reid took to his bed early that night. He'd sent few dispatches to McFarlane, but he drafted one that evening while lying beneath a heavy quilt as the wind howled outside the closed windows.

"It's really simple, you know," Reid remarked aloud after completing his report. "This boy strolls in, looks things over, then signals the others if all's as it should be. They know ahead of time what's coming, and how much. They pick the targets, hit early, and get away fast. It's a clear pattern. And a man who takes to habits can get himself shot!"

The following afternoon Reid sat across a desk from Garner McFarlane as the railroadman read the report.

"It can't be that easy," McFarlane objected. "I won't believe we have a dispatcher who talks about payrolls in saloons!"

"Then he's in on the jobs himself," Reid argued. "Either way, you set the bait, and I'll spring the trap."

"I passed word down to the dispatcher already," McFarlane explained. "There's to be a big payroll delivered to Banwell Junction next Wednesday."

"Cheese is in the trap, all right."

"I'll have a contingent of guards on hand, and I'll wire the local . . . "

"No, you keep your men clear, and don't send any fool

wires. They're clever, this bunch. They'll be alert to telegrams or extra men on hand."

"You don't mean to deal with them all yourself?"

"Don't you think I'm capable, McFarlane?"

"Seems a tall order for any man all by himself."

"Won't be by myself. I'll have a rifle to do most of the work. Tell you what. Come along yourself and see how it's done."

"I will."

"Only come with me ahead of time. We'll leave the train at Sterling, and ride in early so as to be waiting for the Stapletons."

"You seem awfully sure of yourself."

"Shouldn't I be? It's an old game with me. Once I sniff out the scent, get a feel for the game, there's not so much to it."

"You're not hunting rabbits, Reid!"

"Oh, you wait and see them run before you say that."

"They've killed men guarding payrolls before."

"They've shot fool clerks who wouldn't know a Colt pistol from an inkwell. Always before they've known the lay of the land, been in control. You watch how easy it is to turn the table on them. I saw it often enough in battle. Men brave as any you'll know would charge up some hill like wildcats. Then they'd catch a volley in the flank and melt like summer snow."

"I hope you're right."

"Pretty soon you'll know," Reid said, nodding grimly.

Wednesday morning, shortly before daybreak, Copley Reid nestled in the soft straw in the loft of a barn a hundred yards from the Banwell Junction depot. Across the way the schoolmaster was chopping stove wood. The depot was silent.

"You warned them to expect trouble, didn't you?" Reid asked a groggy Garner McFarlane.

"Did it personally when we got here last night."

"Then all that's left is the waiting," Reid said as he swung the Alsweig toward the depot. The telescopic sight focused on the bright red letters *A, T, & S F* stenciled on the sides of freight boxes. At a hundred yards the high-powered rifle would send a bullet slamming into a man with tremendous force. The gun was intended for shooting elk at a half mile's distance. It proved an effective tool for stopping road agents and railroad bandits as well.

The train and the sun broke the horizon in unison. The depot by then had sprung to life. Two freight handlers and the stationmaster were on hand to greet the fictional payroll. No passengers left the train, and the dusty road remained deserted save for children walking or riding to the schoolhouse.

"I don't know that I like having those kids so close," McFarlane complained.

"Be good witnesses, and they're well clear of my line of fire. I don't expect the Stapleton boys to get off many shots outside. You don't want some legend springing up that will spawn a dozen new gangs. How many Missouri boys call themselves Jesse James and shoot up banks? Three Stapletons are enough."

For the first time McFarlane seemed pleased with what he heard. The security director was even more pleased to see the children ushered inside the school. Then the train pulled out, and a heavy silence fell across the scene.

"First the lame boy comes," Reid whispered. As if on cue, the curly-haired young man rode up to the depot, dismounted, and limped inside. Walls and windows prevented hearing or seeing within the depot, but when the door reopened, the young scout puffed his cigar vigorously and blew one, two, and then three circles of smoke.

Moments later, four riders approached. A fifth man followed. He held the horses while the older, taller men continued along inside. Scarcely had the door closed when a pistol shot exploded through the depot.

"Help!" a man screamed.

The children at the school rushed to the twin windows and

peered out as Newt Shanklin kicked open the door and peered outside.

"You first, Shanklin," Reid said as he calmly aimed, fixed Shanklin's unshaven face in the sights, and squeezed the trigger. The rifle whined, and even as the bullet tore through the killer's skull, Reid was busily reloading.

"Lord, Newt, what's happenin' out there?" Tom Stapleton cried.

George did more than call. He rushed outside and knelt over the heartless Shanklin's corpse. The rifle whined again, and a bullet tore through George's back, severed his spinal cord, and left him howling in agony a second before growing eternally still.

"Let's get out of here!" Frank yelled, dragging his stunned brother along toward the skittish horses. Reid tried to steady his aim, but a horse shielded Frank Stapleton. The lame youngster hobbled past as well, and the four survivors managed to get mounted.

"It's not quite over," Reid muttered as he fired a third time. The bullet splintered Tom Stapleton's right elbow, leaving his arm hanging awkwardly at his side.

"Frank?" the younger brother called.

"Ride, Tom!" Frank shouted. "We'll tend you later."

And so Frank Stapleton led the way down the dusty road, westward, toward the open, friendless plain.

"Shoot them!" McFarlane pleaded. "They're getting away."

"Won't for long, McFarlane. There's time."

Down below, a handful of schoolchildren gathered beside the bloodstained road and stared at the stricken corpses of the outlaws.

"Look up there," one boy said, pointing to Reid and the long rifle cradled in his arms. "He did it. Must be some kind of shot."

"Bet he's a Pinkerton," another claimed.

"You figure that's Frank Stapleton?"

"Naw, that there's Newt Shanklin," a tall, sandy-haired boy

of perhaps thirteen explained. "I seen his picture on posters. Other one there's George Stapleton. They're dead, sure."

The stationmaster staggered out of the depot then, and a girl rushed to his side.

"Papa, they didn't hurt you, did they?" she cried.

Reid turned away from the scene. He didn't wish to see tears or suffering. He'd grown acquainted with both in the trying days of youth before the grim, hauntingly real sketches attracted the attention of Washington society. He'd learned well during the war to leave his emotions behind as he sketched dismembered soldiers amidst acres of smoke and blood and gore.

Only the paintings of gallant charges or docile camp life had met with much approval. The nation hadn't been prepared for the chilling realities of civil war.

"Coming down?" McFarlane asked as he climbed down the ladder from the loft.

"When I finish," Reid said, breaking down his rifle into its component parts. Later there would be time to clean and oil the gun. A man, after all, took care of his tools.

"We lost a man," the stationmaster told McFarlane when the security director finally joined the assembly below. "Young Abe Weller, just eighteen."

"Yonder's his brother Billy," the sandy-haired boy said, and a smallish youngster dropped his chin to his chest.

Again Reid shut it all out. There would be no stories of daring bandits bravely fighting the cruel railroad this time. Instead a boy would perhaps talk of the brother now to be missed, and a schoolmaster would relate how shots whizzed past the crowded classroom. No, there would be no glory, in death, for George Stapleton or Newt Shanklin. Only a shallow hole awaited the outlaws.

"I'll authorize payment on these two," McFarlane told Reid when the rifleman finally approached the station.

"There he is," the children muttered. "Is he a marshal? A Pinkerton man?"

"He works for the railroad," McFarlane explained. "He saved us all, didn't he?"

A murmur of agreement followed, but Reid paid little attention.

"I'll be riding out soon," he told McFarlane. "Put the money in the bank. You'll owe me the rest pretty quick. I'm going after the others."

"I could get you some men," McFarlane offered.

"I don't need them," Reid replied. "I've got all the help I need."

He tapped the leather case, then turned back toward the barn. His horse was already saddled, and the animal wouldn't mind a brisk run. The ride over from Sterling had been a short, plodding journey, after all.

Reid paused but a moment. Closing his eyes, he pictured the nervous outlaws gathered around a small fire, doing their best to comfort Tom while they worked on his arm. Frank would likely be vowing vengeance or making plans. Well, there'd be no time for either. Death was again on its way.

"Yes, death," Reid muttered as he spurred his horse into a gallop. "Coming fast."

CHAPTER 4

HOLLAND Sisk fed twigs to a small fire. He couldn't quite believe what had happened. That morning he'd sauntered into the depot at Banwell Junction, expecting yet another successful raid. There'd been just the stationmaster and a pair of freight handlers. Then the freight men drew pistols, and the world seemed to explode. Even then, all went according to plan. Newt shot one of the freight handlers, and the other quickly surrendered.

Yes, it might have been over then and there but for that sharpshooter in the barn across the way. He'd been invisible, a snake lying in the grass until his moment came. Then, before any of them quite realized what was happening, Newt and George lay killed, and Tom was bleeding his life away.

They hadn't even gotten any money. That was the worst part. It was as if the railroad had known, had expected, the Stapletons. But how?

"Who'd figure such a thing?" Frank Stapleton growled from the other side of the fire. "Backshootin' scum. What sort o' fellow kills a good man like George that way?"

"You ever see a man shot in two like that?" Sisk asked as he built up the fire. "Hole big as my fist, Frank."

"Saw a buffalo holed by a Sharps .70," Cle Smith muttered.

"Sharps make more noise'n a cannon," Frank argued. "No, I figure it to've been one o' those new long-range guns, maybe with a spyglass atop it."

"Never heard o' such," Smith said, shaking his head. "A gun ought to make a sound 'fore it kills you. I don't think George even knew he was dead till it happened. Nor did Newt."

"Whatever it was, it leaves a big hole," young Tom said, staring down at his shattered arm. Blood continued to seep through the dressings, and clearly the arm would have to be amputated to save the young outlaw's life.

"Never you worry 'bout it," Frank urged. "You just rest easy. We'll keep a watch. Nobody's findin' us down here."

Sisk agreed. After all, the hollow they'd holed up in was a perfect hideout. Trees concealed the horses, and there was good grass and a sweet spring nearby. Dry, brittle wood and cow chips made a nearly smokeless fire. From the surrounding plain, they were close to invisible. Even a sharpshooter had to have a target to put in his sights, after all.

"Hollie, let's leave the fire awhile," Frank ordered then. "I got a job o' work. Why don't you see if you can tighten those bindin's on Tommy's arm. 'Pears to be bleedin' still."

"Sure," Sisk agreed as Frank walked over beside a scrub oak and began scratching in the nearby sand. Soon the outlaw leader unearthed a small iron cash box. Inside were neat stacks of banknotes, the gang's takings, less expenses, for the past year and a half.

"How much is there?" Tom asked as Sisk fought to stop the bleeding.

"Close to twenty-five," Frank answered.

"Twenty-five . . . thousand?" Smith asked. "Why, we're rich!"

"If we live to spend it," Frank grumbled.

The comment fell heavy on Tom Stapleton, and the young man gazed wearily at the fire.

"Frank?" he called.

"Little brother, I got to finish with this box," Frank said, prying it from the rocky soil.

"I goin' to lose my arm, Frank?"

Frank frowned, then set the box down and returned to his brother's side. Holland Sisk stepped away, then walked to where Cle stood tending the horses.

"What's gone wrong, Hollie?" Cle asked. "Wasn't so long ago we had it all our way. Now . . . "

"I figure somebody must've set a trap for us," Holland explained. "I don't know. Maybe they just got lucky."

"That's one thing I never been," Smith grumbled. "Not since the day I was born."

"Oh, you haven't done so bad, Cle."

"No?" the stocky youngster asked. "You remember how it was at school! Ofus, they called me. Or dopus. I never was smart like some, but there was no call to hang such a name on me. I blame Pa. Bein' the runt didn't help, either. Well, let 'em call me names now. I'll show 'em!"

"Nobody laughs at us now we ride with the Stapletons."

"Nobody," Smith boasted. "'Course, you always found a way o' gettin' on the winnin' side o' folks, Hollie."

"Girls maybe," Sisk admitted. "They always had a likin' for me, I confess. But you can't make a livin' at courtin', Cle. You recall how Mr. Bradley at the mercantile beat me proper for smilin' at his daughter. And then there was that fellow with the knife."

"Yeah," Smith agreed. "Man does that, well, he ought to get his heart cut out."

"If he'd stayed 'round, I'd gotten to it once I mended."

"Sure. Hollie, you think Tom'll mend?"

"Not that arm," Sisk declared. "Lord, Cle, it's close to comin' off on its own. Got to cut it soon or he'll bleed to death, but I'm hanged if I see us goin' into some town to find a doctor."

"It's over, ain't it?"

"Maybe. Well, we had a fair run, didn't we? And there's money to buy land or a store or whatever."

"I'd buy myself a small livery. Or a ranch," Smith said, grinning as he gazed out toward a distant hillside. "I like horses. You can trust 'em to be what you think. No horse ever dealt me wrong."

"Me, I wouldn't mind ranchin'. I'd rather run a little

gamblin' house, though, maybe bring in some girls to entertain, somebody to sing like Ma Totley's got."

"That'd be just fine, wouldn't it, Hollie?"

"I saw some pictures of a place in Omaha, just outside o' town. Had pretty glass all over the place, and the gals wore glittery red dresses, and . . . "

"You boys ready to put a pot on?" Frank called.

"Guess dreamin' can wait," Sisk said, grinning at his old friend. "I'll get a kettle started. You finish with the stock."

"Sure," Smith agreed.

The two of them then scrambled to their assigned duties. It was a little later, when the four surviving gang members collected around the fire to share a scant supper of boiled beef and potatoes, that Frank Stapleton spoke of the future.

"Tom's finished," the elder Stapleton asserted. "He's weak from bleedin', and that arm's got to come off. He needs a doc bad. I got to get him into Hutchinson. We got friends there."

"What about us?" Sisk asked.

"I wouldn't complain of company, but truth is you'd be fools to ride into town when the whole countryside's likely after us. They don't have pictures o' you two yet, so like as not you could sign on some farm or just lay low awhile."

"And the money?" Sisk asked.

"It stays buried. You go spendin' beyond your means, somebody'll get suspicious."

"What about that fellow shot Newt and George?" a feeble Tom asked. "Can't let him get away with that!"

"Don't have any notion who it was," Frank answered. "You can't shoot everybody hangs 'round a railroad office. Be glad he hasn't followed us."

"What if he has?" Sisk asked.

"Then he's a dead man!" Smith barked. "I'm not afraid o' him. We'll ride out and flush him, shoot him dead, and tack his hide to an oak tree."

"Yeah!" Tom said, forcing a grin onto his face.

"You bunch o' fools," Frank countered. "The man shot Newt Shanklin dead and dropped George a minute later is the kind o' fellow you ought to run from. I've seen that kind. Bounty men, some of 'em. Others wear a badge. But their hearts are the same. They love the hunt."

"Hunt?" Smith asked.

"Sure," Frank explained. "They set after men like some track deer or buffalo. They set their traps or ambushes, and they shoot to good effect. This one, well, he's like a wolf settin' after a bunch o' rabbits."

"I'm no rabbit," Smith objected. "I won't run."

"I would," Frank declared. "I've fought men hand to hand, and pistol against pistol, but that devil's got a gun kills from the next county. It's like a hand reachin' out o' nowhere to kill."

"That trouble you?" Smith asked.

"Ought to worry everybody. It's a worrisome thought."

Even Cle Smith had to admit that.

"Let's get some water boilin'," Sisk then suggested, and Smith grabbed a bucket. The two of them set off toward the spring together. They got only halfway when Holland Sisk detected the glint of metal on the far hillside.

"Frank!" he called in alarm, pointing toward the flash.

"Lord help us," the eldest Stapleton called as he rose to his feet. He'd barely pulled a pistol from its holster when a shrill whine drove the others to cover.

"Frank?" Tom cried as his brother made a half turn, then collapsed beside the fire. A swelling circle of red spread across his chest.

"Oh, Lord," Tom mumbled as he tried to scramble to safety. Again the rifle whined, and a bullet sliced through Tom Stapleton's shoulder and punctured both lungs. Tom wheezed a dying breath, then rolled onto his side.

"Let's get out o' here," Cle Smith cried, grabbing what few bits and pieces of supplies he could locate. Sisk, somewhat calmer, raced across the open ground, rolled across the clearing, and grabbed the cash box. As the rifle barked, he raced back to the horses.

"Give me that blanket," Sisk cried, and Smith handed over a frayed Indian blanket. Sisk deposited the cash inside, then tied the blanket neatly and slung it across the back of a tall black horse favored not long ago by Frank Stapleton.

"We can't just leave 'em!" Smith argued, pointing at their dead companions.

"Can't help 'em now, Cle," Sisk said, his face growing pale as he again detected a glint of metal on the far slope. "Best look after our own hides."

Smith took one long last look at the camp, then untied the reins of the speckled mustang he was accustomed to riding. The two young friends then climbed atop horses and rode briskly through the tangle of scrub oak and briars up the far slope of the hollow.

Sisk sought the safety of a small grove of cottonwoods, then drew his horse to a halt. He gazed toward the distant hillside as if half-expecting a dark phantom to appear, gun in hand, to taunt him. Instead, a stumpy, bespectacled man with an odd-looking rifle descended the slope toward the deserted camp.

"Can't be," Smith cried. "Can't be just one of 'em."

"He looks like a schoolmaster, Cle. Got a string tie and polished boots. We could ride down there and lay him low."

"No," Smith objected as the stranger halted. The cold, calculating eyes turned toward the cottonwoods as if they could see through limbs and leaves.

"Cle?"

"Look at them eyes, Hollie," Smith suggested, shuddering as if a chill wind cut through his ribs. "He's smilin'. Lord, he enjoys it. There's no treatin' with a fellow like that! Best we ride—hard!"

"Where?" Sisk asked. "Who'll help us?"

"We got twenty-five thousand dollars here. That'll buy a lot o' help," Smith declared.

"You sure? Seems to me a lot o' folks'd stab a man in the night for that kind o' cash. What we need's somebody we can trust."

"There's just one o' them," Smith said, nervously gazing westward. Sisk nodded, and the two of them set off at a gallop toward a reunion with the one true friend who had never betrayed or abandoned them. They never glanced back. They didn't dare. For it seemed that death was at their elbow, ready to strike quick and hard as before.

Copley Reid stood beside the bloody corpses of the Stapleton brothers for a quarter hour before he brought himself to inspect his handiwork. Frank had been a clean kill. The one shot through the chest had brought a quick and silent death. Young Tom was a ghastly mess. The shattered arm lay twisted and misshapen beneath the young man's body, and blood was everywhere.

"I wouldn't have thought one man could hold so much blood," Reid grumbled as he wrapped the corpse in blankets. Better no one should see the mess an Austrian rifle can make of a young Kansan.

Reid next inspected the ruin of the camp. He went through pockets and knapsacks, blanket rolls and a pair of leather cases. Altogether, he counted a little over a hundred dollars in weathered greenbacks and loose coin. A few letters to girls in railroad towns revealed that Tom had had a poetic side. A ledger revealed merchants who had provided supplies. McFarlane was sure to make use of that! The empty iron cash box was less help.

The loot had vanished, and though there were scrawlings and playing cards, dice and razors, Copley Reid failed to find a clue to the identity of the mysterious youngsters who completed the Stapleton band.

"Should've taken the whole bunch!" Reid growled, angrily kicking a coffee pot across the camp. "Fool! You let them finish their supper. Growing soft, it seems. You had them all here in one barrel, and you let the two get clear!"

Worse, Reid realized, the lame one must have grabbed the cash from the open chest. By McFarlane's estimate, there might be tens of thousands of dollars hidden away somewhere. Sure, let those boys run to hell and back, but the money was another thing altogether.

Reid continued to sift through every bit of clothing—tossed shirts and drawers, trousers and hats thrown about like apple peelings. Then, as he turned a shoe upside down, a small square of yellow board fell out.

"Well, now, this is more like it," Reid said, bending over and raising a small photograph from the ground. In the background was the impressive facade of a grand hotel. *Chester* was neatly stenciled across the large front windows.

"Chester?" Reid asked. "There's no Chester hereabouts!"

But though the hotel was little help, the three faces that smiled across the picture were the answer to a tracker's prayers. The two on either end, though a year or so younger, were without doubt the young outlaws that had managed to escape Reid's snare. The third, a younger-looking boy of perhaps fourteen or fifteen, rested an arm on each of his comrades' shoulders.

Reid turned over the photograph, but the printing on the back had been blurred beyond recognition by age and rough use. Only a date remained legible.

September, 1880. Two and a half years had passed since then, and a mustache now aged the one on the right. They were taller, and a bit older as well, but it wouldn't be too hard for the keen eye of an artist to recall the changes well enough to provide a worthy sketch for the engravers. McFarlane would post the two thieves in every stagecoach depot and train station from St. Louis to San Francisco.

"Won't be a rock you can hide under," Reid promised as he pocketed the photograph. He then walked to where the remaining Stapleton horses were tethered, brought two toward their lifeless riders, and began the grim job of tying the bodies across the saddles.

It was late afternoon when Copley Reid rode up to Banwell Junction at the head of a column of three horses. The two trailing animals and their bloody bundles drew more than a little attention from a knot of onlookers. A schoolboy trotted over, peered beneath a blanket, and pronounced that Tom Stapleton was now among the dead.

"That other one's Frank!" a bystander yelled. "I recollect those silver spurs o' his well enough."

Garner McFarlane met Reid in front of the depot.

"Two got away," Reid mumbled as he climbed down from his horse. He'd never been half the rider his father had intended, and his rump had taken a pounding from the rocky Kansas trail.

"Which two?" McFarlane asked.

"The young ones. Short, sandy-haired one that held the horses, and the lame, smiling one that scouted the stations."

"Well, you brought in the Stapletons," McFarlane said, smiling. "Those other ones won't rob any stations alone. You've done a quick job of it."

"Not through," Reid explained, bending over to let the stiffness work itself out of his back. "They grabbed the money."

"What?"

"Don't worry. I'll track that down for you. Remember, I've got an interest there as well."

"If you retrieve it," McFarlane reminded Reid. "Which way were they headed?"

"West, or maybe south," Reid answered, waving the railroadman away from the gathering crowd. When they were alone, Reid produced the photograph. "We want the ones on each end, McFarlane. And I figure they may just have run to this town. Recognize any of it?"

"Recognize it?" McFarlane asked, laughing. "Why, they've left you a map, Reid. That's the Chester Hotel."

"Says that. What town?"

"Esmeralda, west of Dodge City."

"Esmeralda?"

"Cattle town, near the Colorado border," McFarlane explained. "There's a westbound coming through this evening can have you there tonight."

"Dodge City tonight," Reid said, grinning. "I need to make you some sketches, let you get some posters made up. It's best I arrive in Esmeralda looking my best. I'd judge our friends might find allies in that town."

"Young outlaws!" McFarlane growled. "We'll soon be finished with them. Hasn't been much work for the hangman in Dodge lately. These two will keep him busy a day or two."

Reid ran his fingers along the cold steel barrel of the Alsweig and doubted there would be need of a hangman. Those two were either riding hard for Mexico, or they would turn up in Esmeralda. If the latter, they wouldn't find the refuge and comfort they sought. Only death waited for them, cold and sudden and forever.

"You know it, too, don't you boys?" Reid whispered to the photograph.

There was no reply, of course, for none was needed. Copley Reid asked few questions. He simply stated facts.

CHAPTER 5

THE town of Esmeralda hugged the rails of the Atchison, Topeka, and Santa Fe line in far western Kansas, halfway between the thriving cattle town of Dodge City and the whistle-stop depot of Sherlock. To the south of town, the Arkansas River flowed relentlessly eastward with waters fed by the melting snows of Colorado. East and west the prairie was sprinkled with small farms and cattle ranches.

The story went that when the town was founded by a now-forgotten buffalo hunter named Sanchez, a particularly bright March sun had turned the river into a glimmering sea of emeraldlike green. Inspired by the sight, and lately presented with a bawling baby girl, the hunter named both his encampment and the child *Esmeralda*—Spanish for rare gem. By 1883 the little dugout that had offered shelter to hunters had grown into a sprawling maze of cattle pens, shops, and houses. The population was close to three hundred, and Esmeralda's churches and stores provided a center of life for the surrounding farms and ranches.

To Copley Reid, stepping off the rear coach of the A, T, & S F westbound, the town seemed like a magnet drawing its life from the flat, windswept plain north and south of the Arkansas. Cattle towns might rise and fall, even as Abilene and Wichita had, but Esmeralda seemed to possess a beating heart that would outlast the pens or even the railroad. Prosperity seemed to be etched into the very bricks and planks of the buildings. The townfolk assembled on the platform awaiting friends and relatives were somehow filled with that rare ambition that refused to be checked by fate or circumstance.

Yes, Esmeralda was determined to carve out a future for itself. The town appeared ready to forget its frontier heritage and usher in the bright promise of the twentieth century, still seventeen years away. There were no pistol-carrying cowboys swaggering up front street, no steel-eyed sheriff or stiff-backed judge on hand. Instead, women pushed baby carriages or replenished supplies while men conducted business or enjoyed a bit of distraction in the town's two saloons.

The heart of the community was the brick-fronted Chester Hotel, a three-story structure built of the same commercial pine as every other structure in town. Yet its red brick false front—brainchild of its owner, Aurelia Henley—provided an impression of strength, of permanence in a world fraught with change.

Even if the photograph hadn't marked the Chester as a key in tracking the Stapleton gang's survivors, Reid would have walked to the hotel. Garner McFarlane had spun a tale of its female owner that in itself would have whetted the appetite of any investigator worthy of calling himself the same.

"Widow Henley came to Esmeralda penniless, with four children, and she showered the town with a golden dawning. Aurelia was a Greek goddess, you know," McFarlane explained. "Goddess of the dawn."

"Not Greek," Reid objected. "Roman."

"All the same to me. Anyway, she borrowed money right and left, spent too much on the place, bought fine furniture and feather beds, started serving three meals a day, and all of it with but a dream to guide her. Well, folks responded, and she's probably the most famous widow in western Kansas now."

"Oh?" Reid asked.

"Entertains senators and governors, even the president of this railroad. I can't tell you how many cattlemen have forsworn the goings-on at Dodge City for the comforts of the Chester. Why, she had a Russian prince in this winter, and one of General Grant's boys November last."

"Must be an unusual woman," Reid declared.

"Is that and more," McFarlane readily agreed.

Copley Reid vowed to see for himself. First, though, he had other business to conduct.

In his coat pocket was a letter of introduction to Kermit Donley, the town sheriff. Garner McFarlane had spelled out the details of Reid's requirements, then added a personal message and a promise of generosity when reelection time approached.

"Step easy where Donley's concerned," McFarlane had warned. "He's particular protective of his town and its good name. And I've never known him to be overeager to step past the strict letter of the law in anything."

Copley Reid took the words to heart. He walked into the sheriff's office, set down his valise and the leather rifle case, then addressed a blond-haired young man sitting behind a clerk's desk.

"I have a letter for Sheriff Donley," Reid explained.

"Yeah?" the boy asked, taking the sealed envelope and examining it. "Who're you?"

"Copley Reid."

"I heard o' you, mister?" the young man asked.

"Not likely," Reid replied. "Could you arrange for the sheriff to meet with me?"

"Well, he doesn't see just anybody, you know," the young man said, opening his coat a bit so that a shiny deputy's badge could be seen. "Maybe I could help?"

"Maybe," Reid agreed. "How long have you been in Esmeralda?"

"Four months now," the boy answered. "Uncle Kermit sent for me just 'fore Christmas."

"Then I don't think you'd be much aid," Reid said, losing his smile. "I need some information on some folks used to live here. And I need it now."

Reid's eyes blazed in such a way that the deputy unconsciously drew back in his chair. He then rose and rushed to a small back office. Moments later a compact man of perhaps forty years with thick black hair and friendly green eyes appeared.

"I'm Kermit Donley," the sheriff introduced himself. "You have a letter for me?"

"Yes, sir," Reid said, pointing toward the envelope resting on the deputy's desk. The sheriff snatched it, tore open the flap, and quickly read the contents.

"Haven't had a glimpse of the Stapletons in Esmeralda for years," Donley declared. "We've just got one bank, and they maintain their own guards. The railroad doesn't carry much cash except at cattle market time, and then there are so many cowboys and railroad guards around it'd be pure nonsense to try a raid. Anyway, what makes you think they'd come here? It's Hutchinson seems eager to make those boys heroes."

"Stapletons are dead," Reid explained. "And Newt Shanklin as well. I'm after a pair that rode with them. One's a gimpy-legged youngster with an easy smile and a habit of chasing the ladies. The other tended the stock. He's short of height, but broad-shouldered. I believe they may have grown up hereabouts."

"Oh?"

"I found this photograph in their camp," Reid explained, passing over the yellowing picture.

"They're just boys," the sheriff complained. "You know how many folks have their picture flashed in front of the Chester? Why, Miz Aurelia brings in a man each autumn who does nothing but photograph visitors. They changed the trim two, three years back. It's an old picture. Boys change."

"You might have known them then," Reid said, a trace of impatience finding its way into his voice.

"Look, Mr. Reid, I know you're interested in finding these

boys, but there's no money in it for me. I won't set a bounty man on the heels of a pair of innocents without some proof."

"I'm not a bounty man," Reid objected. "I prefer the title contract detective. I don't chase posters, and I'm certain before I move on a man.

"And you're sure of these two, even if you haven't seen them close up."

"You do know them then."

"I didn't say that."

"Didn't have to. Look, I saw them close enough. The lame boy did card tricks ten feet away from me in a saloon. They're responsible for people dying, Sheriff. Half a dozen in the last year, by McFarlane's count. I promise you they'll have a chance to come to terms. I could probably arrange amnesty even, if they'd turn back the money."

"That's all McFarlane wants?" the sheriff asked. "The takings?"

"You do recognize them, don't you?" Reid asked. "It's the two on the outside I want."

"And the boy in the middle?"

"Could sing in the church choir for all I know," Reid said, grinning. "Only use he'd be is to lead me to the others."

"My eyes aren't what they used to be, you know. Boys pretty much look the same at fourteen or fifteen."

"Do they?"

"Tell you what. If I should happen across somebody looks like these three, I'll send McFarlane word in Topeka."

"Oh, you needn't go to so much trouble. Just have your nephew run the message across the street. I imagine I'll stay at the Chester for a bit."

"Won't find them there."

"Well, you never can tell where a clue's apt to turn up. That picture," Reid said, retrieving the photograph, "was in a boot. Somebody in Esmeralda might have a better memory than you do, Sheriff."

"What is it you really want, Reid? Your name in the papers? A big reward?"

"Oh, I want the same thing you want, Sheriff Donley," Reid said, offering his hand. "Justice."

"Your kind of justice makes me sick," the sheriff grumbled, turning away.

Copley Reid wasted no time leaving the inhospitable office and stepping out onto the street. He'd scarcely taken five paces when a dirty-faced urchin appeared, small pine box in hand, to offer a shoeshine.

"Just two bits, mister," the boy explained. "I can see you're a gent o' quality, likely headed for the Chester. Two bits, and I'll brush the dust off your boots."

"How old are you, boy?" Reid asked.

"Thirteen last month," the boy answered.

"No school?"

"Not for unfortunates like me," the shoeshiner said, putting on a pitiful face as he shook his rag. "Shine?"

"Sure," Reid agreed, and the face returned to life. The boy took out his bootblack and set to work with an energy his thin arms and malnourished body seemed incapable of. As the boy worked, Reid held out the photograph.

"Ever seen anybody resembling these three?" Reid asked.

"I don't get paid to answer questions, mister," the boy answered.

"And if I had a dollar for the right answer?"

"I might find it," the boy eagerly replied. "It's an old picture, you know. Hotel's been changed some. I'd guess it was took two or three years back."

"Two and a half."

"I've seen 'em, all three. Can't remember just where, though. I think the short fellow might've worked at the livery awhile."

"Possible."

"I can't be sure, but I think the one on the other side's

named Jolly or something. He used to hang 'round the saloon some, talk to the girls there."

"And the one in the middle?"

"What's he done?" the boy asked, gazing up with eyes suddenly painted dark and serious.

"Nothing I know of," Reid explained. "It's the others I'm after."

"Then I don't see it much matters who he is," the boy said.

"Not even for another dollar?"

"Not even for ten. Mister, your boots are finished. You can pay me or not, just as you think. There ain't many show kindness to an orphan, and those who do won't find me jabberin' 'bout 'em to strangers."

"Fair enough," Reid admitted, dropping a quarter into the boy's outstretched fingers, then tossing in a silver dollar as well.

"Thanks, mister," the youngster called.

"Consider it virtue rewarded," Reid answered, grabbing his bags and starting across the street.

"Sir?" the youngster called, clearly not understanding those final words. Reid did not tarry to explain.

He stepped inside the twin doors of the hotel, half expecting a dusty sawdust floor and a counter of pine planks and whiskey barrels. Instead he confronted velvet carpets and walls graced by paintings and Italian tapestries.

"Can I help you, sir?" a thin-faced young man of perhaps seventeen asked from behind a front desk of rich mahogany.

If the face had been any other, Reid would have continued his examination of the Chester's lobby. But though the hair was darker, and the lips thinner, the desk clerk's eyes remained the same as when, two and a half years before, they had been captured by a photographer's shutter in the street outside.

"Can I help you, sir?" the clerk repeated.

"Yes," Reid replied. "I'd like a room."

"Certainly. We have several available. Would you care for a

suite, or one of our regular chambers? Each has its own wardrobe and a small sitting room for entertaining guests."

"A regular room would be fine," Reid declared.

"Our rate is five dollars, and we ask you pay the first day in advance."

"Five dollars?" Reid asked, somewhat surprised. The Kansas Hotel in Topeka charged less for a suite.

"The price includes a daily bath, in your own room, change of linens, breakfast and dinner in the dining room, and access to the hotel library. A man of culture such as yourself is certain to appreciate that. Tuesday next, if you choose to stay so long, the hotel will present a reading of Shakespeare by Professor George Randolph Collins of William and Mary College in Virginia. The performance is also free to hotel patrons."

Reid couldn't help smiling. The boy was surely no more than seventeen, a bit shy to judge by first look, and clearly a trifle ill at ease in advertising the establishment in such glowing terms. The hotel itself was far too grand for the town, and they both silently shared the observation.

"You're a fair salesman, son," Reid said, resting his baggage on the floor long enough to draw out his pocketbook. "I'll stay at least a week."

"Well, sir, the weekly rate is twenty-five dollars, and it includes everything I've mentioned."

"No doubt a hair clipping on Saturday as well."

"It can be arranged," the clerk declared. "My sister Edith Ann is our barber, the man in town being prone to strong spirits. I allow her to cut my own hair, though, and she does a fine job of it."

"Well, I'll give that some thought."

"Will you be stabling a horse?"

"No, I arrived on the train," Reid explained. "Where do I sign?"

"Here, sir," the clerk said, turning a heavy volume on its revolving stand. Reid took a moment to scan the names.

McFarlane had not exaggerated. It seemed the entire elite of Kansas had recently visited the Chester. Copley Reid added his name.

"We have three rooms available, Mr. . . . Reid? Copley Reid? The painter?" the clerk asked in surprise.

"I've painted," Reid confessed.

"Sir, I much admire your work," the young man said, reaching out and eagerly shaking Reid's hand. "Well, Mama will faint straight away, Mr. Reid. She's also an admirer."

"Your name, son?"

"Oh, I've clearly lost my wits," the young man said, releasing Reid's hand and taking a deep breath. "I'm Boone Henley. My mother owns the Chester."

"Well, Boone, perhaps you'd do me the honor of showing me around?"

"The honor would be mine," Boone said, setting aside his pen long enough to place the cash in a small iron box. "I'm certain you'll want room thirty-one, at the top of the stairs. The climb can become tiresome, but the view is rather nice, down Front Street and along the river. The light's excellent for sketching or painting."

"You speak as if to know," Reid observed.

"Well, I've dabbled a bit with oils and done some charcoal sketches of friends and family. But it's only a hobby. I'm a poor imitation of Copley Reid."

"Everyone has to start at the beginning, Boone."

"I tell myself the same thing," Boone said. "Just leave your bags at the desk here. I'll have them brought up later."

Boone Henley then led the way down a long hall. He pointed out the dining room, with its great fifteen-foot maple table and silver services. Next came the ballroom, complete with an amazing pivoting stage that converted the flat floor into a theatrical forum. Finally, upstairs, Boone showed off the libary's rich leather-bound volumes of English verse and American prose, Roman discourses and French philosophy.

"Mama brought many of the books over from England," Boone explained. "She says, well, culture cannot be curbed by an ocean."

"Your mother must be a remarkable person."

"Oh, you'll think that and more once you meet her. This whole place is her dream brought to life."

Only then did Reid notice the brilliant oil painting crowning the library's fireplace. Amid a world frozen white with winter's snow, a Shoshoni village came to life in all its myriad colors. The stern-faced women cooked elk strips on a fire while their children huddled together against the December chill. The men gestured wildly as if describing some recent exploit of high drama.

In the righthand corner was scratched *C. Reid, 1877*.

"I did that the winter we returned from the Rosebud," Reid explained. "Was a long, hard campaign, and the bunch of us wound up eating our horses. But we fared better than the Seventh, half of them dying with Custer."

"It must have been a wonder, accompanying the army on such a daring march."

"It was bitter cold and near fatal," Reid remarked.

"Still, an artist has to welcome experiences. I hope to travel to the East one day, maybe go to school there."

"Me, I came west."

"Yes, there is a lot to see out here, but most of the schools teach farming and the sciences."

"And you long for adventures."

"Yes, sir," Boone agreed. "That's it exactly."

The young man then led the way out into the hall, where the two of them were beset by a pair of boisterous blond-haired schoolboys.

"My brothers," Boone explained, grabbing each by the collar and administering a firm shake. "This is Charlie, thirteen, and Jordy, twelve. They're neither worth their weight in salt, Mama says, except if you need to scare rats from the cellar or empty the Arkansas of catfish."

The two youngsters, who resembled each other enough to be twins save for a few inches difference in size, stiffened and offered their hands in greeting.

"This is Mr. Reid, who did the Indian painting," Boone explained to his brothers. "He'll be staying with us a week or so."

"You really chase Indians, mister?" Charlie asked.

"Scalp anybody?" Jordy, the smaller one, asked.

"Mostly I kept a journal and did sketches," Reid told them.

"Maybe later, when he's rested some, Mr. Reid will tell you some stories," Boone suggested. "But not if you pester him with questions. Now get along with your chores."

"Sure, Boone," Charlie said, and the youngsters raced off down the hall.

"Brothers!" Boone grumbled. "It's enough to turn a man to drink."

"I doubt your mama would agree with that."

"No, sir, she wouldn't," Boone readily agreed. "She holds it against a man who takes to spirits to ease his troubles. Oh, she allows a glass of wine with dinner, but she's sent guests packing who brought along a flask or a bottle with them. You won't . . . "

"I'll forget you ever said it," Reid promised.

"Your room's at the top of the stairs there," Boone explained, handing over the key. "If you don't mind, sir, could I ask a question?"

"Certainly," Reid said as he accepted the key.

"You don't paint anymore. I understood you suffered an injury while with General Crook. Frostbite?"

"No," Reid said, laughing. "That story's been about, though."

"Then why?"

"I tired of it," Reid explained. "I found something more challenging . . . and interesting."

"What?"

"Travel," Reid said, nervously shifting his weight from foot to foot. "I journey all over, sending my observations to newspapers, uh, in the East."

"That's always been my dream, seeing new places."

"You're of an age to act on those dreams, Boone."

"I'm seventeen. I've finished all the schooling Esmeralda can provide, and I've read the library from start to finish. But Mama needs my help. Charlie and Jordy, for all their faults, do as well. Our father . . . died years back."

"Sometimes you have to strike out on your own, son," Reid said, swallowing hard. "When I was younger, I had two fine friends who encouraged me to leave home, sell my sketches to newspapers. If I'd stayed behind, perhaps I'd be there yet."

"I had two friends like that," Boone whispered. "The three orphans, we called ourselves, as none of us had fathers, at least not with us. It's been near two years since I've laid eyes on either of them for more than two days in a row. I wonder how they fare sometimes, and I admit to envy. Whatever became of your friends, Mr. Reid?"

"One fell at Winchester, and the other at Antietam Creek," Reid said sourly.

"I'm sorry. I worry my friends will come to a bad end, too, but there's not so much you can do to shape fate, is there?"

"Not much," Reid agreed.

"I'll have your baggage sent up right away."

"I appreciate that, Boone," Reid said, gripping the young man's hand.

The boy then started down the stairs, and Reid began climbing. Room thirty-one was, indeed, at the top of the stairs, and it proved to be as large and fine a place as Reid had hoped. In a matter of minutes, Boone Henley appeared in person with the two cases.

"I saw a leather case like this once before," Boone observed as he refused Reid's offer of a tip. "It's a rifle case, isn't it?"

"Yes," Reid confessed. "I do a little hunting sometimes."

"Buffalo? There aren't so many left here anymore."

"Not buffalo," Reid said, not bothering to mention the real prey he sought.

"Dinner's promptly at six, Mr. Reid. And, sir, we dress for the table. Even Charlie and Jordy."

"In that event, it will be worth the effort."

"Yes, sir," Boone said, grinning. "I know Mama will eagerly await your appearance."

Reid nodded, then closed the door after Boone departed. For his part, Copley Reid couldn't help looking forward to his first meeting with Aurelia Henley. Already a vision of something akin to Queen Victoria surfaced in his mind. He hungered for confirmation.

CHAPTER 6

ASIDE from the fine view of the street, room thirty-one also had a small balcony that overlooked the side of the hotel. It was the fine kind of escape route that wanted men sometimes sought. Copley Reid found it comforting in another respect. By opening the door to the gentle spring breeze, the room soon filled with a refreshing crispness rarely found in the stuffy halls of most railhead hostelries.

There was one surprise yet in store for Reid, and he suspected it was the reason young Boone Henley had assigned him room thirty-one in spite of its stiff climb. Overlooking the big feather bed was a large portrayal in oils of the Rosebud fight. It had always been a particular favorite of Reid's, and he found himself even now smiling with approval at the awesome detail a younger hand had stroked on the canvas.

It wasn't a depiction of the battle as a whole, of course. That disappointed those who expected a panorama, as was the fashion back East. Instead, it was the battle as seen from the eyes of a single soldier, and it showed only three bluecoated soldiers fighting desparately to stave off a charge by a dozen Sioux. Leading them was the fiery-eyed chief with the red hawk in his hair—Crazy Horse. Or so Crazy Horse had been described, for the warrior had made it a practice to avoid photographers at a time when many of the Indian leaders posed proudly for cameras.

Copley Reid, the artist, had lived but a short time after that painting had been finished. Already traces of a new Reid could be detected in the desperate glare of the Indians, in the terrified gaze of the cavalrymen.

"A painter can't portray what he doesn't know," old Josiah Johnson had taught at the Baltimore Academy of the Arts twenty-five years before. Well, Johnson had never created a masterpiece himself, but he'd contributed to the growth of at least one master pupil—Copley Reid. And Reid had never forgotten that realism, above all, was demanded of the artist.

That had kept Reid's paintings out of many a parlor and drawing room. After all, ghastly scenes of bluecoats blasting graycoats, or savage combat between reds and whites, and occasionally blacks, provided a poor backdrop for sewing circles or string quartets. So the Rosebud painting had originally sold to a small Minnesota museum, and other works decorated the halls of statehouses or frontier forts.

"There's a dark side to your work, Mr. Reid," a St. Louis critic once remarked. "It's as if you have embarked on a search for the baser side of man's character."

"A search?" Reid had responded. "Sir, no one need search very far to find the worst side of mankind. It's everywhere."

Reid often wondered if his career might not have taken a different turn had his father's finances not suffered from the risks of land speculation. Perhaps he would have occupied himself painting the portraits of gentlemen farmers or Maryland legislators. But even as a small boy, he had been driven by curiosity, filled with questions about life.

Why, for instance, did some men stand and die while others fled and survived? Was it duty? A call to glory? There was no asking another such a question. To find out, it was necessary to don a uniform and stand in the line of battle, drinking in every sight and smell and taste of the horror that war, in reality, proved to be.

During the war, Reid found himself confronted with the question, haunted by the sea of screaming gray-clad savages charging through the cornfields outside Sharpsburg near Antietam Creek. And he remained for none of the reasons he suspected. He was, instead, transfixed by the confrontation of man against man, by the basic equation that spelled life and death with cold steel and speeding lead.

For some, battle brought a heightened sense of life. The rapid heartbeat and cold sweat drew a man back to the primal struggle, to an absolute reality.

It wasn't until years later, trudging along on foot with the remains of Crook's column toward Fort Fetterman and salvation, that Reid discovered a darker truth. For some men, stalking and killing other humans was the grandest game of all. In spite of its strength and power, even the grizzly provided no challenge equal to pursuing the great thinking creature—man.

Reid recalled bitterly the morning he'd brought Noley Barnes into Wichita slung across the back of a pack mule. Barnes had plagued the railroads and banks of southern Kansas for a score of years. One pursuing posse after another set out onto Barnes's trail, only to lose it in the twilight mists of the haunted plain. Men, women, even children had met their death at the hated outlaw's hands. And yet it had been Copley Reid who felt the sting of words that day.

"Curse you, bounty man!" Sarah Barnes had cried over her husband's lifeless body. "What makes you think you're better than my man? You're worse. You don't steal to feed your family. You kill for the love of it!"

The words haunted Reid then and now. There was truth to be found there. Oh, the killing was as grim a business as Antietam or the Rosebud, to be sure, and no sane man found pleasure in the act. It was the hunt, the chase that held the drama. Killing was merely the ultimate, inevitable conclusion.

For a time Reid stared wearily out the window at Front Street. A lively commerce took place there on spring afternoons, and he alternately viewed children tossing a ball about and a band of men loading supply wagons outside the mercantile. In the end Reid's eyes fell on the scarecrow of a shoeshine boy, hawking buns outside the jailhouse.

"No games for you, eh?" Reid asked, remembering the hard years when he was doomed to dig potatoes for his aunt as his heart longed for the touch of a charcoal and the clear, unblemished surface of a real sketchpad. Instead, he etched figures in the garden dirt and silently wondered how life could grant a man the soul of an artist and the destiny of a farm hireling.

He wondered if that was what had driven the stableboy to join Frank Stapleton. Was that why the lamed youngster had taken to crime? In the end, he swept such thoughts from his mind. They were, after all, irrelevant. The reality was that thieves they were, and they would pay the grave price all outlaws paid.

A bell clanged in the hall, and Reid pulled his watch from his pocket. It was near six. He hurriedly exchanged his shirt for a fresh one, tied his cravat, and grabbed his coat. As he descended the stairs, he managed to get both arms in the sleeves, and he buttoned the coat as he approached the dining room.

"Good evening, Mr. Reid," welcomed a smiling Boone Henley, showing Reid to a place near the head of the table. A small card with his name neatly printed across the front rested on a fine plate of English bone china. Silver knives, forks, and spoons spread out on either side of the plate. A gleaming silver teapot with the unmistakable simplicity of a Boston craftsman rested in the hands of a serving girl, and platters of roast beef and potatoes, complemented by vegetables Reid had half forgotten, stood at the ready.

Charlie Henley stood at Reid's left elbow, fighting the urge to loosen his stiff collar. Boone and the youngest brother were opposite. A tall, stately gentleman in a dark gray suit took station on Reid's right, next to the head chair. That, of course, would be reserved for Aurelia Henley.

If Copley Reid expected an imperial entrance, he was not disappointed. The widow Henley strolled into the room on the arm of Sheriff Donley. But Aurelia Henley was as far a cry from the restrained and portly Queen Victoria as a pumpkin from a carrot. Lithe and gregarious, Aurelia seemed to dance into the room. She welcomed her guests, spoke to most by name, then turned to Reid.

"Ladies, gentlemen," she began, "I'd have you make the acquaintance of Mr. Copley Reid of Washington City. We're delighted to have such a distinguished artist among us. You have all, no doubt, remarked about the painting in our library. It owes its creation to Mr. Reid's talented brush. Join me in saluting him."

There was polite applause. Then all bowed their heads, and a jittery Charlie spoke the words of a short prayer. Then all were seated, and platters of food began making the rounds.

"Welcome to Esmeralda," the gentleman on Reid's right spoke between bites of beef and carrots. "I'm Lindsey Rankin, president of the Arkansas River Bank here in town. What business brings you here? Painting?"

"Maybe," Reid replied. "I often travel to get the feel of the country, to touch the pulse of the people, so to speak."

"Well, there's no town the equal of Esmeralda when it comes to grasping the heartbeat of these United States. It wasn't always so, of course. Not long ago we were just another railhead with cattle pens. Then Aurelia graced us with her presence."

"You're much too generous, Lindsey," Aurelia insisted.

"She brought refinement to our community," the banker declared, and a chorus of agreement sprang up. "She's brought Shakespeare and Mozart to her stage. Mr. Clemens, better known as Mark Twain, gave a series of readings here last year. We might have had Mr. Dickens, from England, had not a fever shortened his last American visit."

"Not bad for a woman who came to town near broke," the sheriff added. "Remember, Aurelia? You passed the first night in the bed of an old army supply wagon."

"That's when she came to me with the hotel scheme,"

Rankin explained. "Well, she had no money, and what manner of a fool would loan money to a penniless widow to build a big hotel in the middle of nowhere?"

"You did, Lindsey," Aurelia said, and the table enjoyed a moment of laughter at the banker's expense.

"Loaned her the funds out of my own pocket," Rankin added. "The best investment I ever made, for she not only repaid the note with interest, she brought prosperity to Esmeralda. First thing you knew, churches were popping up. Stores. A school. We became a real town.

"That wasn't all my doing," Aurelia argued. "Your Martha, rest her soul, had the women organized when the Chester was little more than a brick front. And it was you, Kermit, who rid the streets of handguns."

The assembled patrons of the hotel went on exchanging compliments, but Reid paid them little mind. He emptied his plate and filled it again. Never had he been so thoroughly full.

Later, after enjoying a slice of lemon cake, Reid rose with the others. He might have left the room had not Boone pulled him aside.

"I'd like you to meet my sister, Edith Ann," Boone said, nodding toward a pretty, delicate-featured girl of sixteen. Her long blond hair and fine features were a mirror image of her mother, and Reid suspected broken hearts aplenty would lay in her wake.

"Mama has had me studying art," Edith Ann confessed, "but I fear I lack the aptitude for it. Music is my creative outlet. I hope to study at the Jorgenson Conservatory in St. Louis next year."

"Really?" Reid asked. "Who's to clip the hair when you leave?"

"Boone, you didn't tell him about that, did you?" the outraged girl cried. "Oh, I'll be awhile remembering that!"

"She lances boils, too," Charlie whispered. "Ask Banker Rankin."

Young Jordy laughed a bit too loudly, and his mother flashed a scornful eye toward the boy. Jordy froze instantly.

"Come, meet Mama," Boone suggested, leading Reid through the departing diners toward Aurelia Henley. The widow stepped away from Sheriff Donley and took Reid's hand.

"Pleased to meet you, ma'am," Reid announced. "Your hotel is everything I was led to believe."

"I'm gratified you judge it so," she replied. "To a man who has visited New York and Philadelphia, and toured the continent, our modest efforts must seem very ordinary."

"I haven't spoken of my travels, have I?" Reid asked in surprise.

"Your paintings have brought word of you," she explained. "Prince Maximillian of Bavaria was here last winter, and his cousin, Baron Carl of, oh, wherever was he from, took you hunting in the Tirol, I believe."

"That's right."

"We often have guests who admire your paintings. They portray so much of the dramatic events of western America this century, don't you think? And knowing you paint from actual experience seems to add such weight to the faces and movements of your subjects."

"I feel at a loss for words, Mrs. Henley," Reid said, avoiding her glance. "You have me at a disadvantage. I feel like a small boy who's been spied upon at the swimming pond."

"A fine metaphor indeed," she said, laughing. "In truth, I have followed your career with interest for a number of years. We've met before, you see."

"We have?" Reid asked in surprise. "I can't imagine forgetting such a lovely face."

"I was younger, just fifteen, and newly arrived in America. My Aunt Emily hosted a reception for you in Washington, D.C. That was, I believe, October, 1862."

"I recall the party," Reid said, grinning. "I'd just turned

over my rifle for a correspondent's credentials, and *Harpers* was publishing my sketches of the fighting at Antietam."

"Shocking, ghastly pictures, those, but all the more true, I am certain. And you yourself were young."

"Nineteen," Reid said, grinning. "I told *Harpers* twenty-five, though. Even then, I believe they thought I must be a lunatic to offer sketches as an unknown to a major magazine."

"You had confidence, and the courage to pursue your dream."

"No, fear of being drafted back into the infantry," he said, laughing nervously. "Better to sketch a battle than fight it."

"You didn't appear cautious to me then, nor do you now. I read an account of your gallantry in rescuing a Shoshoni scout while riding with General Crook."

"More like the other way around," Reid insisted.

"But you killed a Sioux from great distance."

"The steady eye of the artist."

"Steady nerve, Colonel Hillman termed it."

"You had Paul Hillman here, too?" Reid asked, shaking his head. "Why, that scoundrel would have you think the two of us climbed the Rockies one day and wrestled Sitting Bull the next. Don't believe half of it, Mrs. Henley."

"I shan't if you say so."

"I advise it strongly."

"Well, we really must speak again soon. I have other guests to visit now. Would you care to gather with the family and friends a bit later in the ballroom? Edith Ann plays a bit, and we occasionally sip a glass of claret and share a few songs."

"I'd enjoy that," Reid told her.

"Then we'll expect you at eight. Perhaps tomorrow night you'd care to share something of your travels. It's been so long since I've had word of England, and my heart longs for it."

"I'll provide the cure, ma'am."

She smiled in retiring, and Lindsey Rankin immediately appeared.

"You say you're considering painting something of the town, Mr Reid?" Rankin asked. "And that's what brings you here?"

Reid nodded. He feared the sheriff might have spread the truth.

"I'd been led to believe you no longer lifted a brush," Rankin declared.

"Oh, I occasionally take on a commission of sorts," Reid explained.

"Private collections, eh? Wise. These gallery agents steal an artist blind, I hear."

"Oh, most are reputable enough. I've benefitted from their attentions."

"I've often thought of commissioning a portrait of my late wife. I have photographs, but they don't bring out her eyes, the fullness of her cheeks."

"I don't do portraits as a rule," Reid said, stepping away.

"Not for a thousand dollars?"

"I generally ask five at least," Reid said without flinching.

"My, I do understand why you work only on commission. Why, only the princes have money to squander in such a way. I believe you're as scandalous a thief as those Stapleton brothers."

"Who?" Reid asked nervously.

"Frank and George Stapleton. There was another one as well. They terrorized the railroad until recently. It's said a single man killed the lot of them."

"That must have been something to see."

"Well, it was a long time coming, but I'll shed no tears for those outlaws. It makes it hard on investments when thieves prey upon the transport services."

"I imagine so," Reid said, bowing slightly, then turning and abruptly leaving the dining room.

Later in the evening he sat in a chair beside the piano

while Edith Ann played jaunty tunes on a wonderful upright piano. A bit later Aurelia led the children in a singalong, and some of the guests joined in. Reid was reminded of such gatherings around the campfires during his army days. Singing often fended off the chills and self-doubts brought on by battle.

There'd been fewer such gatherings in General Crook's command, but for a time while visiting the Seventh Cavalry at Fort Riley, Reid had observed the officers assembling with General Custer to sing away the evenings.

While the guests allowed Edith Ann a brief pause in her labors, Reid sat down and sipped his glass of claret. Boone sat alongside, and Reid found himself recounting his recollections to the seventeen-year-old.

"You've been so many places," Boone said, unable to conceal his admiration. "I would give everything I own to live your kind of life."

"Oh, it's not all you think," Reid confided. "Still, a town like this must seem to choke a young man eager for adventure. It can lead a soul astray."

"Yes, I had a friend said much the same thing, and he, well, I guess it's best not spoken of."

"He was one of the two boys you told me about."

"I told you?" Boone asked in alarm. "Please, don't mention it to Mama. She'd have cross words for me sure. I swore not to speak of either of them. They took some money, you see, and horses."

"I understand," Reid said, reassuring the youngster.

Boone went off to corral his brothers, and Sheriff Donley motioned Reid aside.

"Boone's a good boy," the sheriff declared. "If you've spoken to him at all, you know that. Those other two, well, they left this town a long time ago."

"Recall their names yet?"

"I'll leave that to you contract detectives. You ought to earn your pay somehow."

"And what do you do to earn yours, Sheriff?" Reid asked.

"Protect my town," he answered. "From anybody who threatens her."

Her? Reid wondered if the remark didn't refer to a person, not a town. It didn't matter. Sheriff Donley wouldn't buck the A, T, & S F. In the end, Copley Reid would find what he sought. He always did.

CHAPTER 7

AURELIA Henley found it difficult to sleep that night. Alone, beneath the big canopied bed that had once been of such comfort, she found herself haunted by the shadows of a better past. The lovely rolling hills of her native Cheshire flooded her memory. There, as a girl, she had ridden with her father on summer afternoons when he was on leave from his regiment. How proud and eternal he had looked, that captain of hussars. If only he had not taken fever en route to India, Aurelia might have enjoyed a far different life.

Not that her teenage years had been bleak. There was Aunt Emily's fine house in Georgetown, with gala parties and scores of fine young men. But the war had come along, calling the best of them away and thinning their ranks with its scythelike sweeps of fury. George Holmes, the young cavalry lieutenant, had all but proposed when his chest was punctured by a Confederate rifleman west of Richmond. Boone Forbes had fallen, too. And though he had never spoken promises, he hadn't concealed his admiration for the young English beauty she had been. She'd honored his memory by giving her eldest son his name.

In 1865, when at last the carnage came to a conclusion, Aurelia discovered her mother and aunt both ill. Her cousin and sole other relative, Rachel Ivington, had made little pretense of disguising her disdain of the poor English relation. And so when Charles Hunt Henley had proposed marriage, Aurelia had seized upon the offer as salvation from inevitable poverty.

Oh, it hadn't been so bad at first. Hunt had been generous, and his father's shipping business thrived once the southern rivers were reopened to trade. But Hunt withdrew from the family business the same year Boone was born, and the Henley family came to Texas to raise cattle.

The first years brought a measure of success, but Hunt bought more and more land, gambled a bit too freely, loaned money where a prudent man would refuse, and finally risked all on one daring effort to bring cattle onto the prairies of Colorado. Lightning scattered the herd, and when the crew discovered there was no money to pay salaries, they melted away as well.

Hunt took it all with rare calm. He sold what holdings were left and set off into Kansas to make his fortune over. Then, on a dark night six long years before, he'd found his peace in an early death. Aurelia, with four children and no money, was left to fend for herself.

Well, why not? Hadn't her own mother brought a small daughter across the Atlantic after losing a husband? And Aurelia was shrewd enough to see what all Kansas lacked—the civilizing influence of books and culture. So, using charms developed in Cheshire parlors and nurtured in Washington society, she set about charming Lindsey Rankin out of the money needed to build a hotel. And in creating the Chester out of nothing, she found purpose as well as the means of feeding her growing children.

Oh, she sometimes wondered if Rankin knew how close she'd come to failure. Even now it was all too often a close thing. Only the day before, she and Boone had gone over the account books, noticing with alarm that there was scarcely two hundred dollars in the bank after paying the dairy bills.

Yes, just as the Chester's false front of bricks and glass inspired visitors to envision something grander than reality, so it was that Aurelia Henley's fine gowns and genteel manner often impressed creditors with the soundness of her finances.

While strolling through town, she received the admiring

glances of the other women and paused to speak to Rankin or Sheriff Donley or the mayor. And when she listened to the lovely sounds Edith Ann made on the piano or watched Boone lead a young guest around the dance floor, she approached contentment.

Why had Copley Reid arrived with his fine, handsome face and gentlemanly manner to plague her with a hundred "might have beens"? It wasn't fair. Her life was in order. Now she was beset by self-doubt and regret.

She never did find any real rest that night, for even her dreams were of the dashing young painter. They might have toured Europe a hundred times, wintered in the south of France and taken in the baths at Baden, devoted the opera season to Milan, or perhaps spent a year in Vienna or Salzburg. How unfair that those years had been wasted stirring soup kettles and nursing infants!

She would never have allowed such thoughts a moment's time in the daylight, and when she rose wearily from her bed the next morn, she quickly swept doubt and regret away. Charles and Jordan could never be trusted to ready themselves for the schoolhouse without a motherly nod or two, and Edith Ann had yet to master the art of managing Annie Murphy in the kitchen. Boone, well, he would have the maids setting table or scrubbing linens. He, at least, could be counted upon, for he seemed to have inherited most of his mother's virtues and few of his father's faults.

Breakfast at the Chester lacked the formality of dinner. Most guests appeared, ate, and went their separate ways. Sheriff Donley, who often took his evening meal at the hotel, shared a boiled egg and slice of ham with his nephew at the jailhouse. Lindsey Rankin, though not a guest, enjoyed a full meal with the morning newspaper—even if it was the same news read three days running, as Esmeralda had no independent publication and the posts from Denver or Omaha were sporadic.

Sometimes Aurelia would gather the children in the

kitchen, and they would eat alone or with the cooks. But that particular day Boone had his brothers assembled with Copley Reid even before she arrived in the dining room, so she waved Edith Ann over and joined the little knot of male diners at the far end of the table.

"I hope you had a pleasant sleep, Mr. Reid," Aurelia said as he rose to greet her.

"Quite agreeable," Reid responded. "Best I can remember, in point of fact. It's rare to find any quiet in a railroad town."

"Sheriff Donley keeps a sharp watch on the street," Boone volunteered. "We have a curfew, and the saloons close at ten."

"That must limit their trade," Reid observed.

"Has," Boone agreed. "Once were ten of them. Now just the two, and they're nothing to what I hear they have in Dodge City."

"What's that, Boone?" Charlie asked eagerly.

Their mother frowned, and Boone shifted the subject of the conversation. Soon they were speaking of literature and history. The younger Henleys hurried to finish their breakfasts, then excused themselves. Edith Ann remained a bit longer. Finally her duties with the kitchen staff forced her departure as well.

"I fear I have obligations, too," Aurelia announced, rising slowly. "We will visit again soon, I hope, Mr. Reid."

"I hope so, too," Reid answered, standing. "Be sure to compliment the cooks on their work for me."

"I will," Aurelia said, nodding to him politely. She was, in fact, surprised he should offer such a remark. The food was good and hearty, but certainly no match for the cuisine of Paris or Vienna. As she made her way among the other guests, she felt his eyes following. Well, perhaps she hadn't altogether lost the charms that had drawn young gentlemen's attentions twenty years earlier.

An hour later, while inspecting the work of the morning maids, she found herself drawn irresistibly to the library. There, among the prize books which more than anything drew her back into the distant past, she gazed at the Shoshoni village and wondered how it was that a man who could portray the vitality of those Indians, who could capture on canvas the wonderment of children and the drudgery of weary women, could also paint the horrid spectacle of blood and battle. Even now she recalled vividly his sketches of Antietam assembled for view in her aunt's reception room. Youthful soldiers, many no older than Boone, had cried in silent agony from those charcoal etchings.

Aurelia Henley had grown up a soldier's daughter, had heard her father's tales of glory, but never had she imagined the horror Copley Reid painted as war. The Shoshoni village was reality, she decided. She recognized the smiles and fancies of the children, for she had seen the same on Boone's face, in the mischievous grins of Charles and Jordan, in Edith Ann's attempts at evading chores. Those sketches of war were revelations of some strange, inner madness, she decided.

There was a movement behind her then, and she turned to spy Copley Reid himself, carrying a small notebook of some sort and a large square resembling a map.

"Oh, I didn't mean to intrude," Reid apologized. "I believed the room empty. Your son said I was welcome to . . . "

"As indeed you are, Mr. Reid," Aurelia said. "All the guests are welcome to use the library as a study. I merely stopped to admire your painting."

"I'm flattered. Do you suppose, by the way, that you could do me one very great favor?"

"I will do my best," she promised.

"I'm rather uncomfortable being called 'mister,' " Reid explained. "I'd appreciate your calling me Cope."

"If you can bring yourself to addressing me as Aurelia."

"I believe I can, with great ease."

"I seem to recall our having had a similar conversation twenty years ago," she said.

"We really did meet, then?" Reid asked.

"My aunt gave a reception for you, as I explained. Your sketches were spread out on three long tables, and you stood to one side, I daresay more frightened by the meddlesome women and bubbleheaded gentlemen than by the entire Confederate Army."

"I wouldn't say that. You never heard a rebel yell."

"Next to the howl of three hungry boys, I doubt it would bother me in the least."

"Maybe not," he said, laughing. "I do recall the reception, but I'm afraid little else. I wasn't so old myself then, and the war had scrambled my thinking more than a little. Otherwise I never should have forgotten the lovely girl with the charming English accent you must have been back then."

"Well, you escaped that nicely, Cope."

"A man who travels learns diplomacy."

Aurelia couldn't help grinning at the remark, and he mirrored her smile. For a few moments the mood grew solemn as they spoke of fallen friends and Washington ladies now wed to senators or railroad presidents. Aurelia then spoke of Hunt, of their dreams and the disappointments that had followed.

"And what did you do, Cope?" she asked. "I should have thought you to have your pick of the belles. You went west instead."

"Not for a year," he explained. "I traveled south, painting the devastation as well as the revival of life and spirits. I sketched free slaves for *Harpers* and painted a series of oils on commission for Liberty College in Massachusetts. In truth, the editors weren't very pleased that I portrayed poverty and hardship, and the college refused the oils altogether. I sold them to a private collector for half the promised funds."

"Then west?"

"A Baltimore newspaper offered me a job, and I was in sore need. They sent me first to St. Louis, then up the Missouri. By and by I left their employ, and I wandered to

Kansas, down to Texas, then finally accepted a commission as correspondent with General Crook's expeditions."

"And in all that time, you never . . . "

"Married? Settled down? I admit to being tempted a time or two, Aurelia, but I suppose I was too long on the march, too early. My feet just won't stay still long enough."

"Perhaps you haven't truly offered them a chance."

"Perhaps," he confessed. "There's always tomorrow. As for right now, I'm sure you have work to do. I know I have. Excuse my intrusion again. I look forward to dinner."

"As I do, Cope," she said, stepping aside. He was out the door before she thought to suggest he stay in the library and do his work there. She laughed at herself a moment, for after all he was old enough to do what he wished where he pleased with no need of suggestion from Aurelia Henley. She straightened a volume of Dickens, then left the room and moved along down the hall. There remained rooms to inspect, and Boone had some correspondence awaiting her signature.

Copley Reid had been tempted to pass the rest of the morning in the library, sharing remembrances of Washington and listening to Aurelia's delicate voice enunciate with care each syllable of every word spoken. It was a far cry from the freighters and baggage handlers down at the depot. Even the telegraphist seemed prone to contract three or four words into a single phrase whenever possible.

Yes, Reid might have stayed—but there was a purpose at hand that couldn't be altogether ignored. McFarlane anxiously awaited word on the two renegades, and Reid would soon have to press Boone for particulars.

Or would he? Standing on the street fifty yards from the Chester, Reid couldn't help remembering the brightness of Aurelia Henley's azure eyes. Pressing things might panic Boone. Those outlaws would appear sooner or later. They would wait awhile, wouldn't they?

Yes, he decided, ignoring the pair of telegrams from McFarlane speaking of urgency and crisis. There would be time later. For now, it was best to move slow, cultivate Boone's trust. And as for Aurelia, well, there was no law against passing some time in her company. If the opportunity presented itself, he would be a fool to ignore it.

CHAPTER 8

THE following morning a young freight handler arrived at the Chester with two mysterious bundles, together with a hastily scrawled note from Garner McFarlane.

It read:

Reid—

Congratulations again on dealing so swiftly with the Staple-tons. No word locally on other two. Enclosed are posters as per your instructions. Keep this office informed on your progress. We expect an early conclusion to this matter.

G. McFarlane

Reid offered the boy half a dollar, then showed him out. Once the door was closed, he opened the parcels and discov-ered two stacks of fifty wanted posters. The engraver had done a good job of copying his sketches, and the two faces staring up from the paper seemed real enough to touch.

"Won't be long now, boys," Reid declared as if the outlaws might somehow be able to hear his words. "You're not invisi-ble anymore. Soon the whole state will be after you."

It's said a hunter often feels a closeness with his prey. Copley Reid had never before known that sensation. Just now he wondered what terror might fill those two, hiding in some deserted barn or lean-to out in the hollows of western Kan-sas. Death loomed so near to them, and soon they would realize there was no refuge to be found. He'd somctimes noticed how some animals, realizing they were trapped, would fight tenaciously, biting and clawing even with their dying breaths. Others simply gave up and greeted the end with a silent resolution.

Reid nodded grimly at the posters. The reward spoke of a thousand dollars for the two of them, somewhat less than had been offered when the gang was at large. No mention was made of the accumulated cash, and that troubled Reid. After all, the young renegades weren't altogether stupid. They could outbid the railroad at present, buying silence and safety with stolen dollars. Worse, the money might remain forever buried in some secret hole or jammed into the hollow stump of a live oak, left to rot away over the years.

Well, you'd best find them and the money first, Reid told himself. He grabbed the posters, added McFarlane's note to his accumulated papers stored safely in a disused boot, and set off to deliver the posters to Sheriff Donley for distribution.

Reid wasn't expecting a warm reception from Donley, but the sheriff's response to the posters was blunt.

"I'll tack one up on my wall," Donley agreed, pointing to a clutter of posters near the door. "Anybody wants to look, they can."

"I thought you might distribute them around town."

"No," Sheriff Donley refused.

"Maybe you could loan me a man to ride along the river," Reid suggested.

"I'm not in the habit of loanin' my deputies to the railroad or anybody else. I don't particularly like your line, Reid, and I think you come to town wearin' false colors, talkin' fancy and makin' Aurelia and young Boone think you're such a fine fellow when all the while you're no better than those mangy rawhiders who chase bounties out o' Dodge City! Tell you what. You do your job, and I'll do mine."

"You're sworn to uphold the statutes of this state, and that includes chasing down these killers," Reid argued.

"I never heard how either o' these boys shot anybody," the

sheriff objected. "That poster reads 'dead or alive.' Says nothin' at all 'bout trial. You figure that's justice? I don't."

"Justice?" Reid asked. "Since when did law and justice sit at opposite ends of the same equation? I've seen scant justice in this life, and I expect little. It isn't justice that brought in Crazy Horse or Sitting Bull, penned up the Cheyennes like cattle down in the Nations. It's progress dictates our reality, Donley, sets me after these young outlaws and forces you to join in the game."

"I call my own tune, Reid."

"I'm certain McFarlane will have something to say about that. There's an election here soon, I imagine. Railroad's liable to have some say in the outcome."

"I'm too old for threats, Reid!" Donley shouted.

"Threats?" Reid asked, making a half turn so that the lawman could read the cold manace that filled those hunter's eyes. "I'm a man remembers aid and rewards it. And those who step in my path come to regret it."

Copley Reid stormed out of the jailhouse, posters still in hand, and made his way to the rail depot. He left the posters with the stationmaster, together with instructions that each train through should carry along enough to post at every stop along the line east and west of Esmeralda.

"I'll need a couple of men to ride out and post notices in the nearby towns, at stage stations and taverns," Reid added.

"I'm shorthanded," the stationmaster complained.

Reid only laughed and drew out the crumpled letter from McFarlane that ordered every assistance be offered Copley Reid.

"I want the whole batch up by noon tomorrow," Reid instructed.

"Yes, sir," the stationmaster replied.

Reid didn't halt his efforts there, though. He continued to make the rounds through town, visiting the citizens, gradually bringing the conversation around to one or the other of the young thieves, always taking care to cover the deadly intention of his pursuit.

Reid met with little progress. Most people were strangely close-mouthed, and many had arrived in town too recently to be of aid. Over at the mercantile, though, a young clerk named Clark Hollister grinned broadly when Reid spoke of his association with Boone Henley.

"Boone and I've known each other forever," young Hollister explained. "We were in school together, and I used to wash dishes at the Chester 'fore I landed this job. My folks have a farm just east o' town, and there's fourteen of us kids. Once you get your growth, you got to make your way, Pa always says."

"Then I'll bet you know, oh, I can't recall his name for the life of me," Reid said, pausing. "I spoke with him just a few weeks back, in Hutchinson, I believe it was."

"Who?" Clark asked, the curiosity flooding his face.

"I can't recall the name. Was about your age, though, near too handsome for his own good. He could talk your ear off, have you stepping into a fireplace and thanking him for the chance. Had one leg a bit lame, though."

"Oh, that's Hollie Sisk," Clark said, laughing. "He's a talker, all right. Ought to see him with the girls. Why, when he was twelve, he had half the gals in school after him. Sat down with Pascal Charboneau's wife one night when he was fourteen. That's how come he drags that leg, you know. Charboneau found 'em and grabbed a knife, cut poor Hollie's hamstring. Word was the crazy farmer was tryin' to make a more permanent impact on Hollie, only Charboneau was fond o' spirits, and the leg was all he could reach."

"Trifling with married women at fourteen?" Reid cried in disbelief.

"Well, I don't know it was Hollie's doin' exactly. Miz Charboneau wasn't but sixteen herself, and she had an eye for fellows. Ran off with a drummer two months later, you know.

And Hollie, well, he lost his pa early, and his ma was mostly sick then. She's dead now, too."

"He didn't say so, but I got that feeling. Talked of Boone a lot."

"Oh, they were great friends, as Boone's likely told you. I think Miz Henley was awful glad to see Hollie leave town, as she always viewed him a bad influence. But what's a fellow with no folks to do save work when he can and find mischief the rest o' the time?"

"Yes, life can put some men on a rocky trail," Reid agreed sourly. He then purchased some miscellaneous supplies, presented the Hollister boy with a generous tip, and set off toward the hotel.

That afternoon Reid paid a visit to the town hall. At first the clerk was reluctant to open up his records, but McFarlane's letter worked magic on the old man. Sifting through birth records a decade and a half old, Reid discovered the birth of one Holland James Sisk almost exactly seventeen years before.

So, you're no longer just a face, Reid thought, unfurling a folded poster and neatly printing the outlaw's name below the sketch. Now there's but one identity to discover.

"So, it's Sisk you were lookin' for," the clerk said, gazing over Reid's shoulder. "Might've known. The family's dead, you know, buried years back. Likely it's best his mama never knew he turned into such a no-account."

"Oh?"

"Boy was forever lyin' and cheatin' his way 'round town. Couldn't hold a job more'n a week or two. That boy's bound to come to no good, I always said."

"Did he have any friends?"

"Well, now, as I recall, he was mostly in the company o' young Boone Henley," the clerk said, nodding three times in rapid succession. "Yes, he and Boone were forever fishin' or swimmin' down at the river, swipin' pies from Widow Morgan or settin' off firecrackers under old Jed Norman's buggy. Fine pair they were!"

"Anybody else run with them?"

"Yeah, come to think of it there was one other, though he left town what, three years back?"

"Recall his name?" Reid asked anxiously.

"No, I don't know that anybody ever called him by name. He was an ugly lad, kind o' hunched over and runtlike. Was like somebody stepped on him hard. Always thought so, anyway."

"Why was that?"

"Oh, he worked for old Abner Ryder at the livery. Was his nephew, I think, on his mama's side. Ab's free with a lash, you know. Has a lot o' youngsters down there, but most don't stay long."

"I see."

"You got what you need?" the clerk asked as Reid returned the birth register.

"You've put me on the right track."

"Then I'll bid you good day. I've got to sweep out the office and tend the accounts."

"I'll leave you to them," Reid said, nodding to the clerk and stepping out the door.

Reid wasted no time making his way to the livery. Abner Ryder was there alone, scattering fresh hay and grumbling to himself.

"Good afternoon," Reid greeted the stableman. "My name's Copley Reid. I came to see about hiring a horse."

"Well, that's my business," Ryder explained. "Got that spotted gelding yonder and a bay mare that's gettin' some exercise."

"The gelding looks a little used," Reid observed. "Maybe I'll have a look at the mare when she returns."

"She's the better animal. I readily admit that," Ryder said. "I've got a team o' mules, too, and four or five mustangs, but you look to be a man who rides to a purpose. They wouldn't suit you."

"No, that's true enough," Reid agreed. "And you, Mr. Ryder, look to be a man who is woefully short-handed."

"Well, that's the curse of a man with daughters," Ryder lamented. "My wife's got the boys in school most of the day, too. I hire some youngsters to exercise the stock and help with the feedin', but it's hard to find good help, even among your own family."

"How well I know that!" Reid said, shifting his feet as a tale came to mind. "I got a wire from my sister a few months back. She said her eldest, young Tom, was in need of a position. Well, I set the boy up as my secretary, paid his passage and all. Then first chance he gets, he runs off west, and I'm left with nothing but red marks on my ledger."

"Nephews!" Ryder said in disgust. "I had one here myself a few years back. My sister's runt, ugly child named Cleophus. Should've known a boy with such an ill-conceived name would prove troublesome. I taught him to use a forge, to shoe horses, to work the trade. Cleophus Smith! Damnable child. He broke a riding quirt over my head when he was just thirteen, and a year later he up and run off, takin' with him my best horses. Took up with outlaws, those Stapleton brothers! Curse 'em all, I read now they're dead and buried. Hope to heaven Cleophus is, too. The ingrate!"

"Must have been hard on the boy, leaving his family so early," Reid muttered.

"Wasn't I his family?" Ryder asked. "I fed him, clothed him, gave him leave to learn readin' and writin', go to church. He was like a son to me, and he robbed me blind. I tell you, friend, if I ever lay my hands on his worthless hide, I'll peel it from him like I would a calf carcass!"

"Rightly so," Reid answered in pretended agreement. "Heard of him since he left?"

"Never a word. For the best. Like I say, if there's a God,

Cleophus is rottin' on some Kansas hillside this very moment!"

If there's a God, Reid thought as he turned to leave, I pray he's more merciful than to send another nephew into the hands of this man!

"Don't you want to wait and see the mare, mister?" Ryder called as Reid withdrew.

"Later," Reid assured the liveryman. "I forgot to send a wire."

"Best hurry," Ryder urged. "Telegraphist stops sendin' an hour short o' suppertime."

Oh, he'll send this wire if it's an hour after midnight, Reid thought confidently. In his mind, the words were already composed:

> McFarlane—Trail hot. Names follow. Lame one Holland Sisk. Stocktender Cleophus Smith. Post names as see fit.—Reid

After delivering the telegram to the depot, Reid started back toward the hotel. Soon he would be sitting at the dinner table, perhaps alongside young Boone Henley, hoping the young man would lead him to the elusive quarry.

Reid paused and opened the poster again. The faces retained none of the arrogance, the cunning and greed he had seen at first. There remained only a desperate scowl, the mark of the hunted. And now he, Copley Reid the hunter, wished he had never learned so much. No longer were Smith and Sisk a pair of shadowy outlaws to be dispatched at will. Now they were boys set alone upon the rocky path that comes of orphanhood—a path Copley Reid was well-acquainted with. Didn't he know the sting of a quirt, too? Hadn't he tasted the bitterness of neglect and cruelty?

It was better not to know the prey, Reid decided. There were advantages to dealing death from afar.

CHAPTER 9

THAT night at dinner, Copley Reid again enjoyed the attentions of the Henley clan, especially those of young Boone and Aurelia. Reid had begun to feel oddly uncomfortable basking in the admiring gaze of Boone Henley. After all, the young man was, more than ever, the means to an end.

Aurelia was another matter. Reid hadn't often enjoyed the company of a woman of such culture and varied interests. Too often he'd relied on temporary companionship bought for the price of a fancy dinner or even a few silver dollars. He'd learned early to rely on no one, for reliance led to disappointment and sometimes heartache. Aurelia Henley kindled a rare glow deep within him, though. And as they sat around the piano that evening and sang half-forgotten, foolishly jaunty melodies of a dozen years before, he began to see the world as he once had known it. No longer was life a game of pursue and slay. Now there was warmth once more, and something like kinship.

When Edith Ann at last tired of playing, Charlie drew Boone aside and whispered something.

"I never promised," Boone complained, "and neither did Mr. Reid. If you want a story, ask him."

Charlie stared a moment at his toes before younger brother Jordan nudged him forward.

"Boone said you might share a story, Mr. Reid," the thirteen-year-old explained. "Will you?"

"Likely it's late, and you have beds awaiting," Reid argued.

"They'll wait long enough for a story," Aurelia declared. "If it's not an imposition, of course."

"I do have some work waiting," Reid explained.

"Please?" Jordan said, sitting beside Reid's feet and gazing up with a restrained kind of longing.

"Pa used to spin tales," Boone explained. "The little ones, well, they can hardly remember."

"Yes, it's been a while," Aurelia agreed. A trace of melancholy crossed her brow, and Reid surrendered to their combined wills.

He began by speaking of buffalo herds so vast they blocked the westward migration for weeks at a time. Later he spoke of Cheyenne horsemen and the feats of daring they practiced in battle. In the end he told of the grave hardships endured on the long trail back from the Rosebud, and of the autumn and winter expeditions which hounded and finally subdued the Sioux.

"Must be hard, being hunted," Boone said, frowning.

"Doubly so when there's no place to turn for help," Reid added. "I'd judge that's why most of the Sioux finally came in, that and the hardships endured by their wives and children."

"You didn't paint much of that, though," Boone observed. "You just about stopped, didn't you?"

"I did for a time," Reid confessed.

"Why?" Aurelia asked, and the children crowded close as if the answer might hold some great wisdom not to be missed.

"I sketched what I saw," Reid said, sighing. "I drew death and starvation and despair. Always my strength was an ability to breathe life into my work. Now there was only death. I lost the will."

"But then you went to Europe, saw all the grand sights," Edith Ann said, smiling in a faraway manner. "The monuments and castles must have inspired you all the more."

"No, I found there was death there as well," Reid explained. "Poverty and disease, an aura of hopelessness. I drew emigrants awaiting ship in Hamburg and Cherbourg.

And I knew it was time to turn to another kind of work, one I was better suited for."

"What?" Aurelia asked. "I always envisioned an artist was born to paint."

"Only so long as his eye allows him to see," Reid said, feeling an icy chill swell up inside him.

"So what did you do?" Boone asked, his smile fading. "Write about traveling places for newspapers? That can't have brought much satisfaction, not compared to riding with General Crook and battling Sioux!"

If only I could tell you the truth, Reid thought.

"You didn't altogether stop drawing, though, did you, Mr. Reid?" Jordan asked. "I've seen you scribble things when you sit out on the street."

"Have you?" Reid asked nervously.

"You know, there are some fine places hereabouts you could paint," Boone declared. "It may seem like Esmeralda's dead, but that's not altogether true. There are people and places as alive as any you've ever seen."

"You might show me some of them," Reid suggested.

"Mama, you think you can spare me tomorrow?" Boone asked. "I was thinking maybe we could make a swing south of the river, visit a few of the ranches and some of the farms."

"Tom Red Stone's down that way," Aurelia suggested.

"Had him in mind," Boone told her. "Well?"

"I think it would do you both good to get some fresh air," she answered. "Besides, the horses want a brisk ride."

"Thanks, Mama," Boone said, grinning. "Well, Mr. Reid, shall we leave after breakfast, make a tour of the countryside?"

"Certainly, Mr. Henley," Reid replied. "I'm at your disposal."

So it was that hardly had Edith Ann returned their plates to the kitchen the next morning than Boone led the way toward the livery. Aurelia Henley, it appeared, had other assets besides the hotel. Two of the most notable were the twin black stallions boarded at Ryder's place. Boone hastened to saddle the restless horses, then helped Reid atop one. Moments later both riders set out toward the river.

There were farms aplenty along the river, and there were more farther south, Boone explained. But he led the way westward instead, toward a cluster of weathered buildings, the largest of which had a sign over the door reading *Peabody's*.

"I guess I should have warned you, Mr. Reid," Boone said as he pulled up short. "There are all kinds of folks inside, and they like to talk about old times. Usually some buffalo hunters swap tales, and there was even a Pawnee cavalry scout in last month. It's a rough place, though, and Mama'd disapprove of me bringing you here."

"Rough?" Reid asked, laughing. "I assure you I've been worse places."

"You haven't been inside yet," Boone warned.

"It smells too good to be as bad as I've known," Reid countered. "Lead away."

They rode to a small hitching rack, secured their mounts, and stepped inside. Almost instantly a lovely girl of sixteen or so trotted over, greeted Boone warmly, and led the way to an empty table.

"This is Lucy Whitaker, Mr. Reid," Boone explained. "We grew up together."

Reid grinned at Boone's use of the past tense. The two of them were hardly more than children still.

"Mr. Reid's a painter," Boone went on to say. "Lucy, he's going to sketch some of the people here, maybe draw the tavern, too. He's quite famous. We have some of his paintings at the Chester."

"Well, welcome to Peabody's," Lucy said, slapping Reid's shoulder. "Bring you somethin'?"

"Maybe a glass of beer," Reid replied.

"Me, too," Boone added, and she set off to fetch the

refreshments. Boone took her withdrawal as a cue to begin pointing out the tavern's peculiarities. He also identified the saloon's patrons. Reid studied each face carefully, half of him wishing the mysterious Smith and Sisk would surface, the other half praying they would remain in their hole. They did, and Reid busied himself sketching the tavern, drawing the tense faces of poker players as a contrast to the amused postures of the barmaids.

He also spoke with some of the buffalo hunters, but he learned little from them except that there were dozens of abandoned dugouts between the Arkansas and the Cimarron farther south.

"You've caught that one hunter just perfect," Boone observed as Reid sketched a crusty old-timer. "It's a wonder, how you glance over one minute, then draw the tilt of the head, the way they hold their cards, even the wrinkles on their foreheads."

"Comes of practice," Reid explained.

"I practice," the young man explained, "but it takes me hours of making skeleton figures and then making mistakes before I can produce anything that approaches being taken as human."

"It gets easier," Reid assured Boone. "As anything does once you do it often enough."

Yes, Reid thought. Even killing.

After a time, Lucy brought them tamales and beans for lunch, after which Boone deemed it time to resume the journey. The two companions, artist-turned-hunter and student-guide, rode south and east until they reached a dugout farmhouse flanked by a small hay barn and a stable of sorts.

"Thomas Red Stone lives here," Boone explained. "He's half Pawnee. When Mama began her hotel, Tom oversaw the construction. He's a whirlwind of work and just about the best man, after Papa, I've ever met."

The half-Indian Red Stone was apparently as industrious

as Boone suggested, for he was nowhere to be found near the house. A bit of investigating led Reid to suspect Red Stone might have ridden out westward.

"You sure?" Boone asked when Reid shared his thoughts.

"Tracks lead that way, and they're fresh," Reid pointed out.

"You know a lot about tracking for a painter," Boone observed. "You did say you hunted some?"

"Learned my tracking from Crook's scouts," Reid explained. "I've been fool enough to have forgotten more than any ten men are lucky to ever learn."

"I imagine so," Boone noted. A new wariness possessed the young man, but Reid couldn't tell if Boone was simply unnerved or more likely was skeptical as to whether Copley Reid could find a roof on a rainy day. At any rate, it was Boone who took the lead as they set out to find Tom Red Stone. However, Reid spotted the farmer first.

"Tom, this is Copley Reid," a slightly embarrassed Boone said when Reid stepped down from his horse. "He painted that Shoshoni village in our library, the one you much admire."

"That right?" the Pawnee asked.

"I fear I'm the guilty one," Reid confessed. "If you don't mind too much, I'd like to sit out here and sketch, maybe draw you and your family."

"Long as you don't eat the seeds," Red Stone said, grinning. He then introduced his wife, Marita, and their three children. Of the group, only Hernando was of an age to take much interest, and he was surely no more than seven. The girls, Ernesta and Anita, were preoccupied helping their father.

"Leave it to Tom to start them off early," Boone joked as Reid rested a sketchpad on one knee and began to capture the scene in charcoal. "Tomorrow he'll likely have Hernando digging a new well."

"Watch I don't shackle you to a plow and get a start on that northwest section," Tom warned.

"I run faster than I used to."

"Not that fast," Tom countered. "No white man ever outran an Indian."

"He's right," Reid agreed. "At least not afoot. I've known soldiers to have a hard time even chasing on horseback."

"Do I know you?" Red Stone asked, scratching his thick mane of black hair. "You look familiar to me."

"I have a common nose," Reid said, concentrating on his sketch. All he needed now was for some forgotten half-breed to recognize him for his earlier commerce with the railroad.

"I have a good eye for detail," Red Stone said, "and I'm sure it was somewhere. I did some trackin' a year or so back out of Dodge. Was it there?"

"Mr. Reid's been touring the capitals of Europe," Boone said, laughing. "He rode for a time with General Crook, though."

"Perhaps it was there," the Indian said, nodding thoughtfully. "Isn't like me not to recall."

Nor I, either, Reid thought as he pondered the meeting. For the life of him he couldn't recall a half-breed Pawnee anywhere. But then it was the unseen observer to be feared most of all.

When Reid had completed his sketches of the Red Stones, Boone led the way back toward the Arkansas. They stopped to watch a prowling herd of cattle, spied a couple of cowboys breaking a range mustang, and observed a band of boys from the town's lone schoolhouse swimming away the late afternoon at the river. Charlie and Jordy were missing, no doubt home minding chores, and the hungry look in Boone's eyes while glimpsing the swimming boys bespoke a childhood that had lacked its proper dose of pranks and devilment, Hollie Sisk or no.

Copley Reid knew that hollow gaze. His own eyes looked much the same.

"Must be a fine way to wash off the afternoon dust," Reid said as he sketched the youngsters.

"Wouldn't know about it," Boone said sourly. "Not much time for swimming when you have a job waiting for you back home."

"Some of those boys are farmers," Reid pointed out. "They have chores, too."

"Their duties end. Mine never do."

"I know," Reid said, swallowing a surge of sadness. "I never tell many people this, but I was raised for a time on a farm. My uncle's place. My father lost his livelihood when I was seven, and he never really regained his health. My mother, well, what could she do? She moved in with a distant aunt, helped her with domestic duties. And I slopped hogs and cut feed until I could stand it no longer. Then a friend of my father's, a Washington schoolmaster, took me into his home."

"Taught you to draw?"

"Oh, I was drawing already," Reid boasted. "He saw to it I improved, that I learned about life as well as art. It was a rare gift he presented me."

"What became of him?" Boone asked.

"He and his son were killed in the Shenandoah Valley battling Stonewall Jackson. I found out the same day they discharged me from the infantry, October of sixty-two, after Antietam Creek."

"Sometimes I wish my father had died in battle," Boone said, sighing. "Maybe I could understand that. At least it would be something I could talk about."

"What did happen, Boone?"

"Papa was in Dodge City, drinking up the profits from a cattle sale. He and some other men took to betting, and Papa boasted he could walk barefooted through the stock pens—on the backs of penned-up longhorns."

"Your papa was an unusual man."

"He was a fool," Boone growled. "I heard the others tell

Mama about it. Papa got less than ten feet when he fell. Those longhorns just trampled him to dust, him screaming the whole time. And once he was buried, the banks called every note in heaven Papa had signed. They took the stock, the land, our house, even some of Mama's clothes. If we'd stayed any longer, we'd probably have left that ranch stark naked!"

"People can be cruel."

"Papa was a fool and a dreamer, Mr. Reid. He never had his feet planted on firm earth, Mama told me once. Well, I'm not like that, but neither do I plan to pass all my days as a hotel clerk."

"What are your plans?"

"I'd like to go to school, learn a trade. Maybe, in time, I could even become a painter."

"It's taken me a long way," Reid observed.

"Would it take me that far, do you suppose?" Boone asked.

"Possible. Only you will decide that, though."

"I want so very much to leave, you know. I was half of a mind to leave when Hol . . . when my friends did. They took a road I could never try, though."

"What was that?"

"They didn't exactly keep true to the law, Mr. Reid," Boone said, frowning. "Me, I could never do anything that would come back on Mama. And there are Charlie and Jordy and Edith Ann to consider. Mama plans for Edith Ann to study her music, and that will leave more work than ever at the Chester."

"You can't lead your whole life on others' terms, Boone."

"Nor will I walk on cows' backs," Boone responded. "I can't ignore my obligations."

"None of us can do that," Reid grumbled.

"So how did you manage it, Mr. Reid? When did you know it was time to set off on your own, be your own man?"

"I don't know, Boone, I'm not sure that I can altogether

say that even today," Reid said, sighing. After all, there was McFarlane waiting for results, and Reid would produce them.

"I wonder why it is that the things that are really important are always so hard," Boone whispered as he glanced back at the boys splashing away the afternoon.

"I don't know," Reid confessed. "But it's a rare truth, isn't it?"

CHAPTER 10

WHEN they returned to the Chester, Boone led the horses down the street to Abner Ryder's livery while Copley Reid, sketchpad in hand, entered the Chester Hotel alone. He took but three steps before Edith Ann greeted him.

"Mama suspected you'd be along soon," she said, handing Reid his key. "She wondered if you'd care for a bath before supper?"

"Care for?" Reid replied. "I'd die for one."

"I'll send Charlie up with some hot water then," she announced. "It might take a quarter hour. Is that all right?"

"Wonderful," Reid assured her.

When he completed the long climb to the third floor room, Reid unlocked the door, stepped inside, and immediately set to work marking his map. He noted Peabody's tavern, located each farm or ranch they had passed, and marked the terrain as well as he could. There was soon a knock on the door, and the two younger Henley boys appeared with buckets of boiling water.

"You did want a bath, didn't you, Mr. Reid?" Charlie asked, a quizzical expression filling his face as he set down his bucket. Jordan, the younger, followed his brother's example.

"I suppose I might have had the tub ready, eh?" Reid asked, glancing around until he located the tub in the far corner past the window.

"No, we'll do that," Charlie objected when Reid started for the tub. "I thought the maid might have everything ready's all. Jordy, go fetch some towels."

Jordan turned and raced off to do as commanded. But

Reid noted by the sound of the steps that the pace slowed with every foot farther away from Charlie's side.

"Here, let me help you," Reid offered as Charlie tugged at the heavy wooden bathtub. "Wouldn't want you to strain something."

"Oh, I do this all the time," Charlie said. "I once brought water for a Russian duke, you know."

"That must have been a treat," Reid said, grinning.

"No, he only complained a lot," the boy explained as he poured water into the tub. "Had a tattooed fellow in here a month back, though. He was interesting."

"I could see how he would be," Reid said, laughing.

"Tell you the truth, Mr. Reid, the good tippers are always girls and old ladies. Old ones want to pinch your face some, but they pay for it. And the young ones, well . . . "

The boy spoke no more, just reddened, and Reid laughed again. Jordy returned with towels then, together with a bucket of cool water to temper the bath. The boys stayed only until Reid was satisfied all was perfect, then scampered out of the room. Reid then disrobed and began washing away the trail dust and sweat of the day's activity. He knew the saddle aches would remain a day or so.

The renewing warmth of the bath swirled all around Copley Reid, first draining his fatigue and then filling him with a growing sense of satisfaction. He had been at the Chester such a brief time. Why was it the place took on the feel and scent of home?

As the bath water began to grow tepid, Reid escaped the tub and began rubbing the moisture out of his skin. His sole wish was for one of those big-shouldered Germans who pounded and slapped until every muscle in a man's body unwound. The ones at Baden were famous. Reid sensed the need for one. He'd sat too long in the saddle.

As he dried himself, he noticed, too, that the skin of his arms and neck had taken on a sickly pinkish tint. In June it would have been sunburn. Now it was more like a wind rash of sorts. Those who had known Reid, the campaigner, would have been disappointed to note the effect years of soft life had taken on that once hearty soul.

"You're old, Cope," Reid scolded himself. "Hair's thinned some, and you get the aches riding half a day in Kansas at a snail's pace!"

He laughed, then wrapped a towel around his waist and drew his shaving kit from a small parlor stand. He lit a candle beneath a tin bowl, then poured some soapy water in and gave it time to heat while he made a lather of shaving powder. He was about to apply the razor's first stroke when a knock came at the door.

"Yes?" he called.

"It's me, Charlie, Mr. Reid," the boy answered. "Come to see if you've got some clothes for the wash. Miz Wandsley is here, and she won't be back till the middle of the week."

"Come in and get them, won't you?" Reid suggested, and the youngster opened the door and slid inside. As he collected the discarded garments and took a half-full seabag Reid had left in the bedroom, Charlie straightened the room a bit, set boots toe to toe, and finally offered to set out dinner clothes.

"Anything for a good tip, huh?" Reid asked, grinning.

"Oh, no, sir," Charlie said, shaking his head seriously. "Mama said you might need some looking after."

"She did?" Reid asked.

"Well, you don't have a wife or anybody to do it," Charlie explained. "I think she kind of likes you, too. Hasn't asked any strangers to the singing in a long time. Boone says you might stay a bit."

"Can't ever tell," Reid admitted.

Charlie stuffed the dirty clothes in a single hotel bag, then stood beside Reid and studied the shaving operation.

"Boone shaves, you know," the boy whispered solemnly.

"You will yourself before long," Reid observed, dabbing a bit of lather on the thirteen-year-old's chin.

"I tried once," Charlie admitted. "Boone says I was lucky not to cut my throat."

"Oh, there's not so much to it," Reid declared. Then, almost before he realized it, Reid spread a thin film of soap across Charlie's fuzzy upper lip, then placed the razor in the boy's hand. With Reid guiding Charlie's fingers, the razor soon scraped away the faint whiskers.

"Strange how it feels," Charlie observed as he touched the lip. "Like it's naked somehow."

"You got used to the hairs is all. Whenever I shave off a mustache, I feel a bit bare. It passes."

"You think maybe next time you and Boone go riding, maybe I could come along?"

"That may be a while," Reid explained, rubbing his back, though the ache didn't stop there. "And I'd judge it's up to your mother."

"Oh, she'll let me, Mr. Reid. She worries we don't have a papa and all. I sometimes ride with Sheriff Donley, you know. Not chasing outlaws or anything. Just riding. Sometimes we fish a bit down at the river."

"Ever go swimming with the other boys?"

"Come summer. Now there's school and chores to eat up all the daylight."

"Yeah," Reid muttered, remembering.

"Guess I ought to get along now, else Mama'll be hollering for my hide."

"Here, wipe off the soap," Reid suggested, tossing a spare towel to Charlie. The boy removed the soap, grinned, then returned the towel. Before Reid could locate a dollar for the youngster, Charlie had slid back out the door and vanished down the hall.

At dinner that evening Boone recounted the day's events for guests and family, and Reid found himself merely nodding his approval at the correctness of the report.

"What do you plan for these sketches, Mr. Reid?" Banker Rankin asked.

"Oh, any that strike me special I might paint. Others I may rework. I could blend several into a scene," Reid explained. "I never really know until I do it."

"Appears to be a rather undisciplined procedure," Rankin judged.

"Much the opposite," Reid argued. "Every step has to be precise, and there's no room at all for error. But an artist has to rely on his instincts. He can't always know which sketch will touch his soul. He devotes his life to sharpening those instincts, and he lives or dies by them."

As a hunter does, too, Reid might have added.

That evening Aurelia and the children again assembled in the ballroom. Edith Ann played, and the boys sang with their mother. Copley Reid sat off to one side. His charcoal traced the lines of their faces, captured the brightness of their eyes and the magic of the notes. Even if the paper could not mimic the sounds, there was no mistaking the shared joy. Reid warmed just watching.

So long as Edith Ann played, Reid drew. When she quit, he hurriedly closed his sketchpad and applauded the effort.

"We really lacked your tenor, Mr. Reid," Boone protested. "Tomorrow you'll join in, won't you?"

"Maybe," Reid answered. "Or perhaps Mr. Rankin will return."

"He wasn't asked," Edith Ann said, grinning. "Come on, brothers. We have chores waiting."

The young ones hurried out of the room, pulling Boone along as they went. Aurelia laughed, then slowly made her way to Reid's side.

"I fear you're the victim of matchmakers, Mr. Reid," Aurelia announced.

"I'm flattered," he replied. "And you're to call me Cope, aren't you?"

"Cope," she said, sliding the sketchbook from his fingers and glancing at the drawings. At first she nodded approvingly at the pictures. As she reached the boys at the river, she paused. He thought he might have spied a tear in her eyes as she stared at Boone's solemn brow. Then she turned the page and looked at the Henley family gathered at the piano. Edith Ann perhaps looked older to her. The boys seemed oddly stairstepped, from boy to man perhaps. And last of all she saw herself, young, so full of life, with no trace of the wrinkles she might have noticed crossing her brow or the concern that darkened her gaze.

"When you first came here, I noticed you had changed," she whispered as she returned the sketchbook. "I thought perhaps the war had taken a toll, that like so many you had grown hardhearted and distant. I was wrong."

"You weren't," Reid argued.

"Yes, I was," she insisted. "A hardhearted man wouldn't find the longing in Boone gazing at those boys in the river. It's a gift, Cope, how you see something better in a person and bring it to life."

"I don't see anything that isn't there," he assured her. "Sometimes we're the last to see ourselves, Aurelia."

"Perhaps," she confessed, taking his hand. "I've thought so myself more than once."

"Oh?"

"It's a hard walk, this life of mine. Raising four children alone, building a business, juggling the one against the other like a circus clown, afraid you'll lose the lot of them the next time the wind blows hard. Sometimes I feel the entire universe upon my shoulders, and I'm no Atlas, Cope. I feel so terribly alone."

"I know," he mumbled. "I know that trail, too."

"You've led a life filled with glamor and adventure."

"Have I? Oh, I've been places. I've seen things. Until now I thought it was enough. But it's like an artist who sketches only for his own amusement. Nothing's special if it's not shared."

"Yes," she agreed, resting her head on his shoulder. Then, without either of them quite knowing how it happened, he turned, and they embraced. For perhaps five minutes neither of them dared let go for fear it hadn't happened, that some madness had crept in and taken possession of their minds. In the end they did draw apart, though. And Reid stared at tears running down Aurelia Henley's cheeks.

"Why?" he asked. "Why the tears?"

"Because it's like your drawings," she explained. "Better than it really is. And, too, because of all the years gone by since that reception in Washington, years that might have been shared."

"You have a lot to show for those years," Reid said, opening the sketchbook and pointing at the faces of the children.

"And as many regrets," she added.

"There's time yet, Aurelia. Years."

"Are there?"

"I hope so. I truly do."

She drew him close once more, and they soon found themselves strolling across the expanse of the ballroom. For an hour they silently danced a waltz. Then Reid excused himself, took his sketchbook, and returned to his room.

He gazed at one line drawing after another. As he looked intently at the faces and places that had etched themselves into his memory, he suddenly felt a great urge to paint. In Topeka, stored away against the chance that one day Reid the artist might replace Reid the hunter, were paints and easel, together with a small box of canvases. He grinned at the thought of touching brush to paints once again. Then he hurried down to the telegraph office. A brief wire brought the needed materials to Esmeralda the following afternoon. He took the mysterious bundle to his room, locked the door, and set about transforming the meager room into a small studio.

For three days Copley Reid thought of nothing but painting. He left the room only to take his meals and enjoy Professor Collins's recitations. The remainder of the time Reid dabbed bits of oil paint on a medium-sized canvas. And by and by a face took form. Delicate shoulders appeared. Brilliant blue eyes burst forth, and wondrous golden hair spread its bounty.

Working on the portrait, Reid recalled the half-forgotten peace brought on by work and purpose. An ancient contentment returned. And he smiled broadly with a satisfaction he'd seldom known.

"It's Mama," Boone observed when he stole a glance one morning that next week. "It's marvelous. Does she know?"

"She doesn't," Reid explained, "and you're not to tell. Swear you won't."

"I promise," Boone said, raising his hand as if appearing before a judge. "When will you present it?"

"Maybe tonight at dinner. What do you think?"

"I'll help carry it down," Boone volunteered. "It will cause a stir."

"Good. I'd say this town could use one."

"Yes, sir!" Boone shouted.

Life was rarely simple when it could be complicated, though. So Copley Reid had found it anyway. He was in the midst of buttoning his collar that night prior to dinner when a small knock on the door announced Charlie Henley.

"Come in, son," Reid answered.

The boy slipped inside. He was unusually stiff, and the air of familiarity that had followed their shared use of the razor was strangely missing.

"Come to help with the picture?" Reid asked.

"No, sir," Charlie explained. "Sheriff Donley gave me this for you. Came by special messenger from the railroad, he says."

"Oh?" Reid asked, taking the small, cream-colored envelope. The initials, *A, T, & S F* were printed boldly within a small boxcar in the upper lefthand corner. Below them was printed *Director of Security, Western District.*

"You in trouble, Mr. Reid?" Charlie asked as Reid opened the letter.

"No, of course not," Reid answered nervously. "I've done some work for this gentleman, though. Commissions, you might say."

"Oh," Charlie said, sighing.

Reid held the brief note up to the light and read McFarlane's remarks.

> Reid—
>
> Report progress. The locals in Sherlock say that our friends are in that vicinity. You're close! I await the swift conclusion of this matter.
>
> G. McFarlane

"Bad news?" Charlie asked.

"I may have some work to do soon," Reid explained. "Figure you could locate a saddle horse for me, Charlie?"

"Mama'd loan you one."

"No, I'll need a horse I can ride hard, son, one I won't be needing to bring back every night."

"I sometimes exercise the animals down at Mr. Ryder's place," Charlie explained. "I wouldn't hire one of his. I'll ask around for you."

"I appreciate that," Reid said, drawing a silver dollar from his vest and flipping the coin to the youngster. "Now, I guess I'd best finish up."

"Yes, sir," Charlie said as he left.

The presentation of Aurelia's portrait at dinner that night had the effect Copley Reid had hoped. For once the queen of the table was without words. Boone accepted the picture on his mother's behalf, and Lindsey Rankin helped mount the painting on the wall overlooking the head of the table.

"It's far too generous to be a gift," Aurelia complained to Reid afterward. "I insist on paying for it."

"You didn't charge me for the evening singalongs or the expert guide service provided by your son," he countered. "Take this for the good faith gift it is intended to be, Aurelia,"

Reid argued. "I know how hard it is to accept something, but I expect you to do just that."

"Then I will tear up your bill," she decided. "From now on, Cope, you're the guest of my family. I insist this time, and you will have to accept."

Reid was taken aback, and she grinned broadly.

"But my staying here . . . that's a business arrangement," he argued. "It had nothing at all to do with . . . "

"And are you telling me painting is not your trade and livelihood?" she asked. "Come now. You know the worth of your work. Calculate what a private portrait by Copley Reid would bring at auction, and tell me if I still don't have the better of our bargain."

"It wasn't supposed to be a trade," he complained. "I wanted you to . . . "

"Hush!" she said. "There's to be no more arguing. It's settled."

I wonder, Reid mused as she clung to his arm. If you knew everything, would you be so eager to welcome me into your inner world, Aurelia? If you understood my true purpose, would you hold me so near?

He knew the answer.

Lately, though, Reid had begun to have doubts about that purpose. Even with McFarlane's message burning in one pocket, he felt no urge to hurry the chase to a conclusion. The old fire that had filled the hunter had cooled. Aurelia had chased the scent from his mind.

But for how long? Reid asked himself. He didn't know the answer, and it haunted him.

CHAPTER 11

HOLLAND Sisk rolled over against the hard dirt floor of the dugout and fought to find some rest. Outside a stray rooster was announcing dawn. Holland was half of a mind to shoot the fool bird and have it for supper. Newt Shanklin would have made short work of that rooster. There was a sure bet. Only Newt was staring eerily from the front page of the Hutchinson *Herald,* and his gun was probably on display in the president's office of the Atchison, Topeka, and Santa Fe Railroad.

Cle Smith, on his way back from the outhouse, cursed the rooster as well. Cle wasn't one for rising early, either, and though he was a better shot with a pistol than Holland, he had thrice failed to end the rooster's reign of terror at the Mitchell farm.

Yes, that's right, Holland told himself. Three years of riding the Arkansas, separating the railroad and its customers from their cash, and here he was holed up in an abandoned dugout no self-respecting rat would call home! Back when the Stapletons were running things, the gang moved in style. Once Frank had hired an entire Wichita hotel. They'd each had a fancy room, a whole bottle of Kentucky bourbon, the kind Frank had a particular taste for, and they'd not been shy of company. No, sir. Even Cle had a girl on each arm that night.

Ole Boone would have laughed himself silly. Oh, Boone had his serious side, true enough, but he could enjoy a bit of foolishness as well as anybody. Once the two of them had stuffed Charlie and Jordy in a flour barrel full of horse dung and rolled it down a hill. And there was the time they'd raided Shirley Draper's washing, and she'd had to come to school in her brother's patched trousers.

Yes, those had been some fine times. Lately more and more Holland remembered those days. So long as the gang had been riding the high road, he'd been too busy doing to think. And Frank always did the planning. Now, well, somebody best start considering what path to take. Soon, too.

"Hollie, you gettin' any sleep?" Cle asked as he stumbled through the opening that had once held a door.

"Not with all that crowin'," Holland grumbled. "Enough to wake the dead."

"I been thinkin' that myself," Cle said, sitting at his friend's elbow. Cle scratched a rash on his bare shoulder worn by his suspenders. It had turned hot, and the woolen shirt that had been a blessing that winter had begun to torment the young outlaw.

"Rash still botherin' you?" Holland asked.

"Pure vexation, Hollie," Cle answered. "How you can abide all those clothes when you sleep's a wonder to me."

"I didn't spend my growin' years sleepin' by a forge, remember?" Holland asked. "I near froze my hindquarters in a garret, and passed one whole winter back o' the henhouse. I sometimes figured I'd never get warm, and I don't ever feel the heat at night."

"I do," Cle said, dropping his suspender straps and giving both shoulders a good scratch.

"Truth is, we could use a bath."

"Like the ones we used to get at Ma Totley's," Cle said, grinning. "Lord, there were some fine times had there. Ma, she'd find a backscrubber even for an ugly ole cuss like me."

"Wish you wouldn't talk like that, Cle," Holland complained. "You're not half bad, especially compared to these stupid farmers 'round here. 'Sides, you're young."

"That make a difference, does it, Hollie?"

"Always has for me," Holland boasted. "You stick around,

Cle. The overflow's apt to pour off onto you. Especially with us saddled with all this foldin' money to get rid of."

"Maybe we ought to ride on down to Ma's today."

"Be hung 'fore nightfall," Holland argued. "That little man with the spectacles is sure bound to have that spot watched."

"He's not so much," Cle said, drawing his pistol from its holster and twirling the cylinders. "I could kill him easy enough."

Holland frowned. The only difference between Cle and any other swaggering teenager was that Cleophus Smith would pull the trigger. He'd stand up to anybody. Of all his attributes, the most pronounced was Cle's fearlessness. It would surely get him killed one day.

"I'm not sure that fellow with the fancy rifle's human," Holland finally said. "Newt was dead 'fore we even knew anybody was there. Was the same way with Frank. Poor George is the only one who really suffered, him and Tom."

"Must be a buffalo rifle he uses," Cle declared. "Close to took Tom's arm off. I wouldn't want to catch a bullet from that gun."

"Nor would I. Truth is, I don't see nothin' but shadows out on this accursed plain, though. We're near starvin'. Every time we go anywhere for supplies, we find these fool posters."

"That's the Lord's own truth!" Cle barked. "How'd they make pictures look so much like us anyway? You figure somebody gave 'em a description? Maybe Ma Totley or somebody in Hutchinson?"

"Doesn't matter," Holland observed. "They got 'em. We must be as popular as apple cobbler nowadays. I mean, I didn't even get inside the depot over at Newcastle when that fool deputy pulled a shotgun and blew the door apart. Another inch to one side, and he'd have spread my best parts over half the state!"

"They spotted us up at Sherlock, too. I figure we best get to movin' soon, Hollie. Posse's bound to set on our trail."

"Isn't posses worry me," Holland said, sinking his chin in his hands. "It's that little man with the big rifle. You can outride a posse, lose it or outlast it even. Can't outrun that gun. It reaches out and kills you a quarter mile away."

"Maybe we can go to Mexico."

"Cle, that'd mean crossin' the Nations and most o' Texas. Two men no older'n us travelin' alone makes a temptin' target for those who ride the Cimarron, not to mention Mexican bandits. Those posters keep us from crossin' the regular ways."

"We've got to go somewhere."

"I know," Holland confessed. "Soon, too. I don't see but one choice."

"Boone?"

"He's smart, Cle. He'll know what to do. Maybe we can give up some o' the money."

"And how do we let him know we're comin'?" Cle asked. "Can't just ride down and shake his hand."

"Lucy Whitaker can get word into Esmeralda easy enough."

"They'll have posters there, too. Hollie, my uncle's not apt to be a lot o' help. He spots me, he'll run straight to the sheriff."

"He won't. We'll go early, 'fore sunrise," Holland explained. "Miz Henley will help out with food and a place to hide while Boone figures things. She never held with hangin' boys, you know, used to talk 'bout it often."

"They've got a lot o' reward on those posters."

"Miz Henley's rich."

"Boone ain't."

"Boone'd cut off his fingers 'fore he'd see harm come to either of us!" Holland cried, springing at his companion and pinning a knife blade to the stronger Cle Smith's throat. "Take that back, Cle, or we part company here and now."

"I didn't mean it," Cle said, breathing easier after Holland withdrew the blade. "Lord, you got yourself touchy, Hollie."

"Must be that rooster."

"Sure," Cle agreed. "He'd make a fine supper, eh? And I could do with somethin' 'sides griddle cakes and ham fat."

"Me, too," Holland announced. "What would you say to a ride out to Peabody's?"

"It'll be watched, too," Cle warned.

"Who's to notice a couple o' more drifters in that place? Especially young ones. Can't tell Lucy what to say to Boone if we never see her."

"You sure that's all you got in mind?"

"Well, it's only natural she shows me how much she's missed me."

"You forget her pa's out to shoot you?"

"Well, you got to take risks, after all."

"One o' these days, Hollie, you'll get more cut than a hamstring, messin' with all these girls at the same time."

"Maybe so," Holland said, laughing. "But I can't for the life o' me think of a finer way to go, Cle. Can you?"

"Maybe not," Cle answered.

The two young men laughed heartily. Then they pulled out rifles and took a few halfhearted shots at the elusive rooster. Finally, after burying the cash in the floor of the dugout, they stuffed their pockets with banknotes, saddled their horses, and headed for Peabody's tavern.

Holland led the way. He, after all, had been born to lead while Cle was born to follow. To both, the broad, windswept plain south of the Arkansas was familiar. The deserted Mitchell farm was just three miles south of the river, and Peabody's place was a couple miles south and east of the farm.

Nobody that worked the tavern could recall who Peabody had been. For as long as Boone Henley could recall, Elmo Whitaker had run the place. Before that there had been a saloonkeeper named Stocker, or Stockbridge perhaps, who had had the misfortune of challenging a dozen Cheyenne raiders back in the mid-sixties. Whitaker had buried what remained of the fool and taken over the tavern thereafter.

Peabody's would never make anybody rich, but if a man worked at it, watered his spirits some, charged Colorado goldfield prices, and had daughters to tend bar, deal cards, or cook food, he could make a decent living. Old Elmo had four daughters, a pair of boys to chop wood and tend fields out back, and the prudence to stay out of the card games that occupied most of his customers.

Holland Sisk and Cleophus Smith need not have felt out of place at the tavern. Three other occupants also rode the Kansas plain with prices on their ears. Two were wanted for helping themselves to stock belonging to others. The third had recently carved up a gambler who, it turned out, was married to the sister of the circuit judge for the western district of Kansas.

Of the other customers that huddled in the dimly lit tavern the morning Holland made his appearance, most were out-of-work cowboys or former buffalo hunters turned rawhiders. They all awaited the coming of the summer herds up from Texas.

When Holland limped into the adobe structure, he inspected the place for recognizable faces. He next gazed at each occupant's boots. Frank Stapleton had often remarked how a lawman will give away his presence by wearing clean, well-polished boots. Holland took such lessons to heart.

He wasn't just wary of sheriffs and little men with spectacles, though. He hoped not to confront the tall, broad-shouldered titan of a saloonkeeper, Elmo Whitaker.

"I'll skin you inch by inch if you so much as look at my Lucy ever again!" Whitaker had warned a few months earlier. Holland didn't have so much skin that he could spare any, and he deemed it wise to spare himself anguish whenever possible.

"Well, here's fresh blood!" a heavily bearded mountain of

a gambler proclaimed as the two newcomers moved past. "Got any cash you'd care to contribute to the game, boys?"

"Boys is right," a seedy-looking cowboy declared. "These two can't be but just escaped their mama's nest. Fresh is one thing, Boley, but these ones're greener'n grapevine in April."

"Care to find out how green?" Cle asked, squaring his hips and peering down his nose at the talkative cowboy.

"No offense meant, friend," the cowboy said, nervously sliding his chair back from the table. "Only meant to spare you some losin'. Boley's got all the luck in this place today."

"Maybe I'll change that," Cle said, taking a vacant seat. "I have a bit of luck my own self."

"I'd say so," Boley, the big man, observed when Cle piled greenbacks beside his elbow. "What'd you do, rob a bank?"

"Done some diggin' in the Black Hills," Cle said, straight-faced and fiery-eyed. "So you see, we're none too green for the likes o' you."

"Tell me that when the game's over," the cowboy suggested.

Then Boley took out the cards and began dealing. Holland, meanwhile, sought out a dark corner. There, with his hat down over his eyes, he waited for some hint of Lucy. It wasn't long in coming.

Lucinda Whitaker, tall, high-hipped, with a shade darker complexion than average, wore her raven black hair long and loose about her shoulders. She was far too lovely to be wasted on Peabody's, Holland had remarked more than once, and if not for her feared father, Lucy would no doubt have fled to greener pastures long ago. She and her sister Rose manned the tavern in their father's absence, and it was actually Rose who approached Holland.

"It's me, Hollie," he whispered. "Send Lucy over."

"I will," Rose agreed. "You just look out for Papa. He's been ridin' 'round lookin' for you. There's a reward posted, you know."

"Sure do," Holland confessed. "So will everybody else if you say it that loud."

"Sorry," Rose apologized as she hurried to tell her sister. Lucy sprang to the back table, gave Holland a quick kiss, then sat with him for a few minutes.

"I need help," he whispered.

"You need a new face," Lucy declared. "Fast as I can pull down these fool posters, somebody else tacks 'em up. They want you bad, Hollie. Did you kill somebody?"

"Worse where the railroad's concerned," Holland said, frowning. "We've got a pile o' their money."

"Hollie, I told you it would come to no good. If only you could've waited a bit, hung on like Boone."

"Boone'd gone too if his Mama wasn't still alive."

"Boone wouldn't ride with a baby murderer like Newt Shanklin. He shot a seven-year-old boy in Newton durin' a holdup. I've got a brother's just seven, you know."

"That's all finished now," Holland assured her. "Cle and I got money, loads of it. All we have to do is get away from here, maybe to California. We'll change our names, start over. Lucy, come along, will you?"

"I've waited a long time for those words," she said, hugging him tightly. "Just let me get my things."

"No, not now," Holland explained. "First, I want you to tell Boone we're holed up at the old Mitchell place. You know where that is."

"I ought to. Cora Mitchell was my cousin, remember? Was me first showed it to you."

"Tell him to meet us out there tomorrow mornin'."

"Hollie, how am I to let him know that? Papa won't let me get into town today."

"Sure, he will. Find a reason. Do it, Lucy. My neck's hangin' on it."

"All right," she relented. "Anything else?"

"A sack o' food wouldn't hurt."

"That'll cost money, o' course. Papa checks on it, too."

"Ten dollars enough?" he asked, pulling out a handful of bills.

"Two's plenty," she said, peeling off a pair of banknotes. "You be sure and go back the long way, hear? That Boley's a bounty man, I understand."

"I'll leave him room," Holland promised.

Lucy brought a food sack, together with a platter of tamales and a cool glass of beer. Holland sat down to eat and watched Cle struggle against the more experienced card players on the far table. It was an unfair contest, but then Cle had plenty of cash to lose.

"Looks like you've had more success diggin' nuggets than drawin' cards," Boley observed after a time.

"That's 'cause nuggets may lie on a hillside or in a stream, but they don't go to movin' about on you once they get dealt," Cle explained.

"Meanin'?" Boley asked.

"You cheat, mister, plain and simple."

"And you figure to call him on it?" the cowboy asked, reaching toward his pistol. Cle was up quick as a cat, and he slammed a beer mug across the back of the cowboy's skull. The cowboy collapsed into his chair, and the other players retreated, leaving Boley and Cle Smith to face each other across the table.

"Give it up, sonny," Boley warned. "I was shootin' men in saloons 'fore you was born."

"Likely so," Cle said, narrowing his eyes. "Man can grow old and fat rememberin'. Me, I've not shot too many men, so it's still somethin' new . . . and fun."

That was one of Frank Stapleton's favorite lines. It always had an unsettling effect. Boley's forehead beaded over, and the fat man seemed unsure of himself. In Esmeralda Kermit Donley would have broken up such a quarrel before blood was spilled. Out at Peabody's, no one would interfere. Cle had done all the backing he was going to. His stiff spine related the news. Boley, whether from pride or arrogance or some great unfathomable unknown, drew his pistol. Cle Smith, the blacksmith's nephew and all-around misfit, pulled his Colt and shot the gambler through the heart. Boley fell back with a clamor, and Cle turned to see if any of the others cared to join in. When none did, he holstered his gun, collected his winnings, and stepped toward the door.

Holland gave Lucy a reluctant parting look, then followed his companion outside.

"Lord, Cle, you do know how to get yourself noticed," Holland pointed out.

"He was cheatin'," Cle explained.

"And now we're all three of us likely killed. Come on! Let's get shed o' this place!"

CHAPTER 12

IT wasn't in Boone Henley's nature to rise with the sun. That much he had in common with his two old friends. For seventeen years first his mother and later Edith Ann had shaken him into consciousness. Now Charlie and Jordy had inherited the task.

"It's morning, Boone!" Charlie cried.

"Get up!" Jordy added.

Finally, as always, a brother took each leg, and they dragged Boone out of the comfort of his bed.

"It's too early," he claimed when he rolled onto the hard wooden floor. "Get washed, then come back."

"It's time," Charlie said, grabbing an arm and tugging at Boone. "Come on, Boone. Work's waiting."

Finally Boone's eyes blinked open, and he grabbed a brother in each arm. Soon the three of them wrestled around in a pile of flailing hands and feet. Then their mother called from the hall, and all three struggled to their feet.

"You boys up?" Aurelia Henley called.

"Yes, ma'am," they spoke in unison.

"Let's hurry it up," she urged. "There are duties waiting."

"Yes, ma'am," they answered again.

While Charlie and Jordy smoothed sheets and folded blankets, Boone shook the cobwebs from his brain and did likewise. It was a wonder that the three of them could get dressed, comb hair into place, and get the room in order in so few minutes. Then, after Charlie and Jordy collected their schoolbooks, Boone straightened a collar, smoothed out a few strands of restless blond hair, and finally led the way down the back stairway to the kitchen.

When they reached the bottom step, however, a slender, dark-haired girl stepped out and blocked the way.

"Lucy?" Boone cried in surprise.

"I need to talk to you," she whispered, glancing back as if someone might be listening.

"You two go along," Boone told his brothers. Charlie and Jordy grumbled a bit, then grinned. Only when they had disappeared into the kitchen did Lucy speak.

"I brought you a message," she told Boone.

"A message? Lucy, what in . . ."

"It's from Hollie," she explained. "Be quiet and listen. He and Cle Smith are holed up at the old Mitchell place. You're to meet them there."

"I am?" Boone asked with widening eyes. "Me? Why? How do they expect me to . . ."

"Boone, I can't stay," Lucy announced, cutting his questions short. "You know how Papa watches when I come into town."

"Lucy, you can't just give me this kind of a message and say nothing. They're wanted, you know."

"All I know is that they're our friends," she said sternly. "I came, didn't I? Hollie'd do it if you were the one needed help. Go or stay as you will, Boone. Only know they're boxed in, and if you don't help, Lord knows what will happen next."

She turned and left then. Boone remained with the burden placed squarely on his shoulders. His first impulse was to shout out the unfairness, curse Holland Sisk for pulling him into a mess like this. But Lucy had chosen her words well. Boone believed Holland would come if the roles were reversed. And so there could be no ignoring the summons.

Boone barely nibbled at his breakfast that morning. He spoke only when directly addressed, and he seemed to lack the energy for even the smallest errand.

"Mama, I may need to take one of the horses for a time,"

he said when the diners began leaving the table. "Figure you can cover the desk this morning?"

"If there's need," she answered. "Boone, is something the matter?"

"No, everything's fine," he declared. "I just, well, feel the need for some air."

"All right," Aurelia Henley agreed. "But if something's troubling you . . ."

"I'm perfectly fine," Boone asserted.

Nevertheless, he stepped out into the hall and paced back and forth anxiously. Even Charlie and Jordy, whispering about a secret romance, failed to distract him from his concerns. They soon sped off toward the schoolhouse, toward the security of lessons and lectures. Boone wished he could find refuge in such a regimen. In the end he spied Copley Reid climbing the stairs.

Boone followed without really thinking what he would say or do. And when the artist entered the library, Boone did so as well.

"Mr. Reid?" the young man called.

Reid turned and nodded.

"You look troubled, son," Reid observed. "Something the matter?"

"Well, in a way, I suppose," Boone confessed. "You might say I have a decision to make."

"A hard one?"

"Yes, sir. You see, I've got an old friend who's, well, got himself in a tight spot. He's asked for help, and I . . . well, I just don't know what to do. I was hoping you might have a suggestion."

"Seems to me you're on the right track, Boone. It usually eases a man's problem to share it with somebody. Only don't you think it'd be better to sit down with your mama?"

"She's got her own worries," Boone declared.

"We all do," Reid pointed out. "But I'd judge she would want to know."

"I can't tell her."

"There's me," Reid said, sitting on the edge of a table and gazing intently into Boone's eyes. "Why don't you start from the beginning, let me know what's happening?"

"It's not as simple as that," Boone said, rubbing his hands together. "It's a trust of sorts, and I dare not betray it. In a sense I have lives in my hands."

"Sounds to me like your friend's put you in a tight place, too," Reid complained. "This the boy you told me about left town a few years back?"

"I told you about him?"

"Oh, a bit, as I recall. Trouble has to do with the law, does it?"

Boone started to lay it all out, but something stopped him. Maybe it was the urgency he remembered seeing in Lucy's eyes or the dread Boone himself felt when imagining something might go awry.

"Boone?" Reid asked. "I can't help what I don't understand."

"I know," the young man admitted. "I wish I could tell you. I really do, Mr. Reid. I wish Papa was still here, too, but he isn't. I'll be eighteen years old soon. I guess it's time I start settling things on my own."

"Boone, young men sometimes make mistakes," Reid warned.

"I know. It scares me, too. But I think I'd better deal with this on my own."

Reid shrugged his shoulders, and Boone left the room no closer to a solution than when he'd entered. He wandered downstairs and strolled through the wide halls of the hotel, hoping some solution would come to mind. It seemed like a bad dream. How long had it been since Hollie Sisk had visited? A year and a half at least. Often Boone had hoped Holland would appear to announce he had parted company with the murdering Stapletons, that he had found a new, better path. Now, when Hollie did return, his name and face were nailed to every depot wall and jailhouse in western Kansas.

What do I do? Boone asked himself. He has no right to bring his troubles down on me and my family! But who else was there to turn to? As boys, they'd faced trouble square in the eye, dealt with each trial side by side. Even when Hollie had lain on old Doc Shaver's cot, lamed for life and bleeding half to death, Boone hadn't turned away.

"And I won't now," Boone mumbled, realizing there was nothing else he could do. So he promised his mother to return before dinner, then set off toward the livery to draw a horse. He would meet Hollie and Cle at the Mitchell place after all.

It was neither a long nor a difficult ride to the Mitchell farm. Boone Henley knew that country well, and the terrain proved little challenge. As he rode, though, he couldn't escape the sensation of impending peril. He constantly felt eyes on his back. It was as if someone was following, and yet whenever Boone doubled around on his trail, there were no tracks or hint of anyone following.

"Lord, I'm spooked, and nobody's got posters with my face on them," Boone remarked as he wove his way through the low hills on the edge of the Mitchell property. "It must be a nightmare being chased, hounded like a rabbit chased by dogs. I warned you, Hollie."

Boone made a final circular swing before approaching the dugout farmhouse. Cle Smith stood in the open doorway cradling a Winchester rifle. Holland waved from the front window. Boone then dismounted and left his horse to graze while he joined his friends inside.

"Wasn't sure you'd come," Holland said, pulling his old friend close. "It's good to see you, Boone. Look at you! You've gone and got tall."

"Well, you're some changed yourself," Boone countered. "You, too, Cle. Of course, it's no secret what you two look like. The law and the railroad stick up your picture about every ten feet. So, what'll you do?"

"We kind o' hoped you might have a notion or so yourself, Boone," Holland replied. "Me and Cle, we've ridden south and west, even east a bit. All we find is men ready to claim a reward."

"They're offering a thousand apiece for you now, I hear," Boone explained. "That's a lot of money."

"Sure is," Holland agreed. "Only we've got more. And if it's needed to get us away from this place, then you just say so."

Holland spread out the cash, and Boone stared in disbelief at the stacks of greenbacks. But instead of seeing those dollars as his friends' salvation, Boone saw only that the railroad would be relentless in recovering that cash.

"Hollie, maybe you can make a deal with them," Boone suggested. "Turn in the money, and they might grant you an amnesty. I hear it's been done elsewhere."

"We need that money," Cle complained. "You figure we've near got ourselves killed for fun? No, sir, we'll never go back to sweepin' stables or sloppin' hogs! I'd rather die."

"That could be the choice," Boone argued. "And there's no guarantee the railroad'd make any deals."

"They got a shooter stalkin' us, you know," Holland broke in. "He plans on killin' us, Boone."

"Then there's no time to waste. Give me some of the cash to take in. I'll see if they agree."

"I said before," Cle declared, pounding his fist against the table. "You can't give 'em the money. It's mine."

"If you've made your mind up about that," Boone said, frowning, "there's nothing I can say. I don't know how I could help."

"You're smart, Boone," Holland said, staring out the door toward the distant Rio Grande and far-off Mexico. "You'll think of somethin'. It's the only chance I've got."

"I don't see what else I can do to help!" Boone claimed.

"Maybe he plans to collect that reward himself," Cle said, staring at Boone through wary eyes. "Wouldn't be the first time a man's sold out his friends to make a bit o' change."

"I hope you didn't mean that," Boone answered angrily.

"He's a little out of his head," Holland apologized. "It's this shooter. He's not human, Boone. We were down at Banwell Junction, rollin' along just fine. Then three shots come from nowhere, and George Stapleton's dead, Tom's got his arm close to shot off, and Newt Shanklin, mean and fast as any man ever alive, is a pile o' bones."

"We thought we gave him the slip, Boone," Cle took over. "Then that rifle opened up again, and all that's left is Hollie and me. We been on the run ever since, and it don't look any too good just now. You got to help us!"

"Look at me!" Boone cried. "I'm seventeen. I mind a desk at Mama's hotel. What do I know about running from the law, about getting past posses or bounty killers?"

"You got a way o' sortin' through things," Holland said confidently. "I trust you, Boone. We can saddle up and ride south for Mexico right now. What do you think?"

"Got any supplies?" Boone asked.

"Got two cold biscuits and a tin o' beans," Cle announced.

"There aren't many trading posts down south not watched by one bounty man or another, I'll bet," Holland stated. "It's rough country, too, with maraudin' Indians and renegade whites aplenty. Cle and I talked some on it, but it would appear a poor choice."

"Best way would be to get aboard a train, make a lot of miles in a hurry," Boone advised, "The trouble is, I suspect the rest of the depots have you two postered all over the place just like the station in Esmeralda. You could ride west, maybe catch the train in Colorado."

"That trail's moderate hard with decent rains and nobody chasin' you," Holland complained. "Guess we could cut up north, follow the Platte along into the Rockies. They've struck gold up on the Yellowstone, I've heard."

"If they have, it'll be gone 'fore we catch up with the place," Cle judged. "Still, I heard there's good land up that way. We could buy a lot o' acreage with all our cash."

"We'd still have to get there," Holland pointed out. "So, we're not any help to you, Boone. Can't you figure anythin'?"

"Well, maybe there is a way," Boone said, scratching his chin. "Could be that you could try a disguise. You could get on the train as a couple of women even. I heard it being done by prisoners escaped during the war."

"Can't hide my leg," Holland said sadly.

"And I don't plan on dyin' in a dress," Cle muttered. "But we could dress ourselves up, grow beards maybe."

"That's better," Holland said, grinning.

"Or maybe you could join the theatre company Mama's bringing into town," Boone suggested. "I've seen those troupes come and go a dozen times. They have these big wardrobe trunks where a dozen men could hide. And nobody pays them much attention when they're not on the stage."

"You think it could really work?" Cle asked.

"Don't know why not," Boone answered. "It'd mean coming into Esmeralda a day ahead, but you could hide in that old shed back of the hotel. You remember the one, Hollie. We used to hide you in there when you ran off from the farm."

"I remember all right," Holland said, his eyes growing dark.

"So how do I get you word?" Boone asked.

"You don't," Holland answered. "I'll get it to you, either by Lucy or somebody. You just keep your eyes and ears open. That way we'll know what's happenin'. You'll hear from us. I promise you that."

"Then I guess I've said all there is to say," Boone told them as he rose. "Best I get along back before somebody gets curious and starts looking for me."

"You look kind o' nervous, Boone," Holland answered. "Why's that?"

"I've never helped an outlaw before," Boone answered, doing his best to make light of the matter. He failed, and Holland frowned.

"You know I never had any choice," Holland complained. "I was near killed at fourteen by a lunatic! I'll tell you somethin' about those Stapletons, too, Boone. They weren't always happy with how I did everythin', but they never shorted me my equal share o' the take, and I was always welcome to share a table with 'em. Can't say that for everybody."

"And now you're paying a price," Boone argued.

"Now I'm rich!" Holland barked. "Money can buy a new name, a new future."

Can it? Boone asked himself as he started toward the door. It changes nothing that's truly important.

He fetched his horse, mounted, and then rode briskly back toward Esmeralda. Again he felt some mysterious onlooker peering from the distance, but the sun sometimes played tricks on the sandy landscape. Perhaps it was just a mirage. Boone hoped so.

CHAPTER 13

SHADOWING a youngster was more than a challenge, Copley Reid decided as he trailed Boone Henley across the flat Kansas plain. There were too few trees, a scarcity of ravines and hills. To do a proper job of stalking, some cover needed to be at hand, and south of the Arkansas, there just wasn't enough.

To top it off, Reid had never become the horseman his father had sought. As a child, he had ridden well enough to stay atop his mount, but by age ten, young Copley was exiled to his uncle's fields, where the only horse apt to come his way was a lead-footed plow horse or a swaybacked mule.

Once, at school, Copley recalled suffering a terrible humiliation at the hands of a batch of Virginia dandies. To those boys, riding was second nature, and they had alternately taunted and tormented their frail Maryland companion. It was all good fun, they announced, and Copley should not take it to heart. Well, that wasn't always possible when you were fourteen, and Cope Reid had retaliated by fraying the cinch ropes of his persecutors. What was meant to be another case of good sport went sour when one of the boys broke a leg.

For several days young Copley spoke to no one. His dreams filled with the episode, and he was plagued by guilt. Then the others accused him of the crime, and he struck back.

"It's time some of you learned not to bother me," Reid had warned. Afterwards he was left to himself more and more, and his pictures became his voice.

It's strange, remembering that, Reid thought as he trailed farther behind young Boone. Such memories were thought laid to rest long ago. Not so, it seemed. Well, perhaps if better ones had come along to take their place, that would have happened. But the hard trials of youth had merely led to a bitter harvest.

A couple of miles south of the river, Boone seemed to realize someone was following. The youngster glanced back periodically, then began making a slow turn back onto his path. Reid spotted a low ridge up ahead and set off in that direction. Hidden among a stand of cottonwoods, he watched Boone play a skillful game of twisting and turning until he satisfied himself no one trailed along.

"Works better in the open, son," Reid whispered. Then, as if by sorcery, Boone Henley vanished.

Boy, where did you get to? Reid wondered. Was it possible that Boone had cut back again and found some ravine to shield his movements? And was he that very instant coming around from the flank?

Reid considered his options. Perhaps Boone was meeting with the outlaws just ahead, scheming to evade the watchful eye of the hunter. Or maybe Sisk and Smith waited on the next rise, rifles in hand, to slay the stalker. At best Reid ran risk of discovery. Once Boone knew the truth, he would never lead anybody to his friends.

Why change the plan now? Reid asked himself. You're close. The boy almost told you everything this morning in the library. Better head back to town and wait out the game. You'll have your chance.

Actually, Copley Reid rode well to the west before turning north toward the river. It wouldn't do to meet Boone on the trail. And Abner Ryder was a famous gossip, and the liveryman was certain to inquire about the ride. Reid took out a sketchpad and drew a section of the plain. Later, he sketched the river, an abandoned dugout once frequented by buffalo hunters, and a pair of women hanging wash on a clothesline.

By the time he approached town, Reid found the schoolboys again enjoying the creek, and he spared a few moments to observe their antics. Those boys, after all, seemed to belong in a different world than the one that sent Boone riding alone across the plain and had Reid following, searching, hunting.

"Water's just fine, mister!" one boy finally called from the water. "Come on in and join us!"

Others waved encouragement, but Reid only waved farewell and headed on toward town. When he rode up to the stable, he met with a surprise. Charlie and Jordy Henley were busy brushing the hire horses.

"Been riding, Mr. Reid?" Charlie asked in surprise.

"A bit," Reid confessed as he dismounted.

"I'll take him," Jordy offered, grabbing the reins. "You look like you've given him a good run of it."

"We covered some miles," Reid admitted.

"Must have been up near Pool Hollow," Charlie said, touching flakes of red clay accumulated on the animal's hooves. "That's a good place to swim. Some of the boys go there in the afternoons."

"Boone showed me when we went out last time," Reid explained. "I was back there this afternoon, doing some drawings."

"We go there some when school's out," Jordy explained. "Too much to do nowadays."

"Glad to hear it," Reid said, grinning at the boys. "Can't entirely grow up proper without a dip in the river now and then."

"Maybe you can talk Mama into a picnic," Charlie suggested. "I'll bet you could."

"Sure," Jordy agreed. "We could catch some fish, fry 'em up with a few potatoes, and have a real feast of it."

"I don't see your mama being talked into anything she doesn't want to do," Reid declared. "But I might mention it just the same."

"Mama loves to go riding, too," Charlie advised. "Isn't

smart going out by yourself, either. Snake could scare your horse, and you could fall."

"There've been outlaws around, too," Jordy added.

"I'm certain they'd run at the mere sight of your mama," Reid remarked, laughing.

"They would if she took after them with a switch," Jordy assured him. "Besides, Charlie told me about that pocket pistol you carry."

Reid frowned. So, fewer secrets remained than he thought. Perhaps Boone knew more than he admitted, too. Reid took a deep breath, then let it out slow. Charlie, meanwhile, sent his younger brother off to strip the saddle from the weary horse.

"Didn't mean to talk about it," Charlie said, frowning heavily. "Especially after you helped me with the razor and all."

"I never intended it as a secret," Reid replied.

"I only wanted Jordy to see a fellow can paint pictures and not be a coward. He didn't believe you fought in the war, that you rode with the cavalry."

"What difference does the pistol make?"

"Lots," Charlie said with serious eyes. "Sheriff Donley doesn't let anybody carry a gun in Esmeralda now, but just about anybody who leaves town straps on a pistol. You didn't. It's good to know you had one."

"Why? Charlie, guns kill people, you know."

"I know," the boy answered angrily. "I've seen it, twice the first week we got here. Sometimes you have to kill a man, like when he's threatening your family. You ever do it?"

Reid gripped the side of a stall and tried not to respond. He felt an engulfing darkness descending, and he tried to cast it from his mind.

"I knew you had," Charlie said. "Sheriff Donley told me once the fancier the gun rig, the less likely the man with it's ever shot anybody. He says to read a man's eyes."

He's right, Reid thought.

"Next time you decide to take a ride, do ask Mama," Charlie said, setting aside his brush a moment. "She's partial to horses, and she doesn't ride much at all now Papa's gone."

"I'll keep her in mind, son."

"And when you're out there, don't forget about the picnic."

Reid grinned, then nodded. Charlie gave a whoop, then hurried to share the news with his brother. Reid paused only long enough to leave three dollars in Ryder's rental cup before hurrying back to the hotel.

After a thorough scrubbing and a visit from barber Edith Ann, Copley Reid descended the stairs and joined the other guests at dinner. Banker Rankin presided over the evening's conversation, which centered successively on the federal debt, the southern Democrats, and Senator Kingman's new wife. A pair of visiting congressmen from Tennessee soon took issue with the banker, and the pale young visitor at the foot of the table just so happened to be one of the senator's new brothers-in-law. In no time voices raved and tempers rose.

Reid kept silent through it all. He hadn't eaten since breakfast, so naturally food seemed more important than senators or even their wives.

"Weather's been most pleasant of late," Rankin finally noted as if to bring the conversation down to a calmer pitch.

"Sure was," Charlie spoke. "Mr. Reid went riding out toward the river, drew some pictures."

"Oh?" Aurelia asked. Reid couldn't tell whether she was more surprised that Charlie had spoken at the dinner table or that Reid had gone riding.

"I took a ride today, too," Boone said nervously.

"Oh?" Reid asked in pretended surprise. "I noticed you gone, but I had no idea you were riding. When did you leave?"

"Just after breakfast," Boone explained.

"We must have just missed each other," Reid said, shaking

his head. "A shame, that is. You were an excellent guide last time out, Boone, and I fear I didn't find nearly as interesting a group of subjects by myself. But then I suppose you may have had better company."

"Himself," Charlie said. "Wasn't anybody else."

"Well, Charlie," Reid said, grinning at Boone. "A gentleman doesn't always leave in the company of his lady. Sometimes they have a rendezvous."

"Mr. Reid, please!" Edith Ann said in pretended shock. The whole table roared, and even the Tennesseans seemed to regain their good humor.

"You know, Mr. Reid," Boone began, "there's somebody else around here who also knows this country. Might make even a better guide, too."

"I stay busy enough, thank you," Sheriff Donley said, and the table enjoyed a second laugh.

"I meant Mama," Boone added. "She loves to ride, too, and I'm certain she'd enjoy showing you the countryside."

"I'd be honored, ma'am," Reid said, nodding toward Aurelia.

"If that's a serious invitation, I heartily accept," she told him. "I'm afraid I also stay busy in the mornings, but perhaps tomorrow afternoon you'd care to have a try."

"Love to," Reid said, though in truth he feared he would find himself outclassed by his companion.

"Then I'll meet you in the lobby at half past noon?"

"Wonderful," he agreed.

They walked together to Ryder's livery that following afternoon. Reid knew he was in trouble when he saw her high riding boots and ivory white riding trousers. Aurelia Henley walked with purpose, and he imagined she rode with a will. He was not mistaken.

Aurelia proved to be a horsewoman of rare talent. Even contorted sidesaddle, she combined a sense of grace and style with energy and control. There wasn't a hint of the delicate creature her narrow hips and trim middle would have suggested. And once set in motion, there was no catching her.

"You needn't hold back on my account, Cope," she told him time and again. "My father had me riding before I could walk. He was a captain of hussars and a master of horse."

"My father rode well, too," Reid explained. "He did not, however, pass all his good traits along to his son. I consider my objective to be staying atop the animal. If I do, I can outlast its antics."

She laughed heartily, then motioned toward the east and set off at a gallop. By now Reid was totally lost. His choice was either pursue Aurelia or risk passing his remaining days wandering in the wilds of southwest Kansas.

He caught up with her at the edge of an apple orchard. Being spring, the bright blossoms danced in a faint breeze, seemingly ushering in a foreign beauty to the bleak plain.

"I once thought to plant apple and peach trees by the dozens in back of the hotel," Aurelia explained. "We would have had a garden in back where the guests could walk and visit, like the one my home in Cheshire possessed. But the climate is dry, and other businesses crowded in so that I had to be content with flower boxes."

"Maybe when the town grows, you can insist on a big park nearby."

"That's a fine idea," she declared. "Cope, does it seem odd to you that such a flat, colorless country should grow wheat and corn as tall as a full-grown man?"

"To everything there is a purpose," Reid said, recalling one of his mother's favorite scriptures.

"I envy you yours. To bring beauty and wonder into the world is the life I would have wished for myself. Instead I rent chambers to strangers and those who don't wish to operate a home for themselves."

"If that's all you did, perhaps it wouldn't be enough," he objected. "But the Chester's more than a hotel. In a way, it's family, too. The imported chandelier in the dining room, for instance."

"It's the subject of a scandalous fraud, I fear. I bought it from a New Orleans amusements palace which had fallen upon hard times and limited finances."

"And the library?"

"Why, that was as much for me, for the children, as for anyone."

"Aurelia, every town needs a heart, and your hotel provides a center for Esmeralda. The same sense of style and culture you present to the town is being mirrored back. There's control, order."

"And if I want more?"

"What?"

"I'm not entirely certain. Something of what you talk of when you describe Paris and Vienna. Grandeur. Tradition. Majesty."

"It's all imagined, of course," he told her. "People make up a town in Kansas or a European capital. It's the quality of the people that makes a community."

"You may be right, Cope, but those other things are there as well."

"If they are, I never saw them. All I found was layered formality and austere smugness. I was invited everywhere and welcomed nowhere."

"They hurt you."

"No one's been able to do that since I was a child," Reid retorted bitterly. "But neither did they show me anything better than what I found in the snowbound villages of the Shoshonis up in the Wind River country, or on the bloody wheatfields near Antietam Creek. If anything, life here has a raw intensity, a purity that draws us to it. It's why your counts and dukes journey here. They hunger for its crisp reality. And in the end, it frightens them to death."

"You believe that?"

"It's a truth. And if you're honest in your observations, you'll have to agree with me."

"I said once before you see something better in people than what is there," she whispered. "Maybe I was wrong after all. It is there perhaps, deep down."

"I pray so, Aurelia, because if not, we must begin to despair."

She smiled radiantly, then turned her horse and led the way slowly past the orchard southward across the plain. As she directed his attention to this farm or that, to a great mound of buffalo bones or an abandoned pile of planks that had once been a railroad work camp, Reid imagined each in its heyday and sketched accordingly. Finally they arrived at Peabody's tavern.

"Care to join me in a sip of brandy?" he asked as she pulled her horse to a halt so that the animal could drink from a nearby pond.

"In there?" she gasped. "It's a most unsavory place, Cope."

"Boone took me here," he explained. "It provided some colorful characters."

"No doubt," she said, coughing. "I'll have to speak to Boone."

"Don't be harsh with him," Reid advised. "It was my search, after all. Besides, boys have to find their own way sometimes."

"Especially those without fathers," she added. "It's been a hard road indeed, Cope. Too hard, I once feared. I thought to take another husband, but there wasn't anyone . . ."

"Strong enough?"

"Oh, Kansas is full of strong men," she answered. "No, I was looking for someone gentle enough to understand that my boys might not always meet a stepfather's expectations."

"And you found no one?"

"Once I thought I did," she said, sighing. "But he was just another dreamer, doomed to die a cold, desperate death one Dakota winter."

"I'm sorry."

"Don't be. I've done rather well for myself. And Boone has been my strong right arm these last years."

"He's a fine young man."

"He's eager to try his wings, though. How lost I'll feel when Boone goes off to school!"

"And Edith Ann is leaving soon as well?"

"September next, whether Boone stays or not. Charles will be next. Then Jordan. The pages turn too fast sometimes. I was weaning them only yesterday. And now you've shown Charles how to use a razor."

"You learned of that?"

"I'm their mother, Cope. They talk to me."

"It was probably Sheriff Donley's job, or Boone's. I fear I stepped into another's place."

"Yes, but it wasn't Kermit Donley's, or Boone's, either. I think it was right, you doing it as you did. You felt the need in Charles, and you responded."

"Or I felt the need in me."

"You? And here I thought you were the man who had no needs."

"Whoever led you to believe such tripe, Aurelia?"

"You did," she explained. "A dozen times I've reached out to you, but even as my hand approaches, you pull away."

"Maybe," he confessed, watching his horse satisfy its thirst.

"I fear I've bent your ear this afternoon," she apologized. "We should be started homeward."

"I've enjoyed the ride," Reid assured her. "And the talk."

"Perhaps we'll do it another time," she said softly.

"Actually, I promised to propose a different excursion. Your sons request a picnic. How does that meet with madam's approval?"

"It sounds delightful," she said. The solemn gaze melted away, replaced by a glimmering smile.

"Then maybe we can come out to the river, say on Saturday?"

"Saturday it is," she agreed.

CHAPTER 14

THERE was something appealing about sharing Saturday with the Henleys down at the river. In his brief time at the Chester, Copley Reid had rarely seen the five of them together except for the brief evening gatherings in the ballroom and at mealtime. A picnic seemed almost too ordinary an activity for Aurelia Henley, and Reid wondered if the children would know how to devote a whole day to swimming or fishing.

As it happened, his concerns were for naught. Edith Ann and a friend from town, Patience Framm, occupied themselves plucking flowers and doing needlepoint. Later they set off upstream and tried their luck at snagging catfish.

Charlie and Jordy spent their morning swimming and fishing and annoying their sister. Boone did his best to herd them back into the river whenever they threatened to overwhelm Edith Ann, and she struck back herself by snatching their clothes.

"Got yourselves in a fix, eh?" Reid called to Charlie and Jordy. The youngsters sat in the shallows, nervously searching for the neat piles of shirts and trousers stacked upon shoes and stockings.

"Edith Ann, huh?" Charlie asked. "You think there might be a blanket handy, Mr. Reid?"

"Might be," Reid answered. "You know, you've been a bit of a vexation to your mama this morning, and it doesn't always profit a man to push his sister too far. If somebody found you some trousers, I don't suppose you'd promise to leave Edith Ann be this afternoon, would you?"

"Gladly," Jordy declared.

"Me, too," Charlie agreed more reluctantly. Reid then rummaged around in the brush until he located the missing clothing. Soon the boys were rescued from their predicament.

Aurelia then called a truce. She ordered boys east, girls west, and warned of the dire punishment to follow the next infraction.

"Sorry, Mama!" Charlie and Jordy called from the river.

"I'll watch them better," Boone pledged.

"In truth, I'm almost relieved," Aurelia confessed to Reid afterward as they spread out blankets in preparation for lunch. "There's been too little laughter in their lives. It's rather pleasant to watch them being young once in a while."

"Yes," Reid agreed, opening his sketchbook and showing her the latest drawings. Edith Ann's eyes were wider and brighter, and even Boone seemed to have lost his solemn gaze for once.

"Even little Jordan's growing," Aurelia said, sighing as she examined the pictures closely. "They don't stay small for long. I'm glad you suggested this, Cope. It has been a tonic."

"It wasn't my idea," Reid reminded her. "The boys brought it up."

"They felt the need, too. I wonder why they didn't ask me on their own?"

"They see how hard you work. They surely didn't want to seem like shirkers."

"It's getting so that they don't seem like boys," she told Reid. "I'll have to remedy that."

She smiled brightly, and Reid felt a strange warmth flood his being. He caught Charlie pointing to them and knew the picnic hadn't been just a scheme to elude work or bring the family together. Copley Reid was the subject of a plot.

"Beware the matchmakers," Aurelia whispered.

Reid failed to reply. Deep down he didn't really mind. It felt good, that growing closeness, the new sense of belonging.

Reid couldn't recall a time when there had been anyone to belong to. He'd been set adrift too early.

"Do you mind a personal question?" Aurelia asked a bit later as they arranged two trays of meats and cheeses.

"If I mind, I won't answer it," Reid countered. "Fair enough?"

"Certainly. I'm not one to pry needlessly, but I can't help wondering why you've never married."

"Is that a question?"

"I'm afraid it is."

"Then I regret to say I don't know the answer. Perhaps there isn't one. I wasn't close to anyone growing up, Aurelia. I had no real family, and few friends. In the army, I learned better than to take anyone to heart. Most soon moved on or were killed. Later I was forever drifting about, living a few months someplace before heading elsewhere."

"You've been good with the children," she observed.

"They've been good for me. Nothing much to that, I suppose. They don't expect much, so they aren't disappointed."

"Cope, I've given a lot of thought to the future since our ride. When Boone leaves, I'll need someone to help run the Chester. It's more effort than one person can . . ."

"Please stop, Aurelia. You're about to say something you'll come to regret. You don't know me."

"Don't I? It may be I'm the only one who has ever truly known you."

"You're wrong," he said soberly.

"Have I misinterpreted something? Did I read more than was there?"

"Not more," he said, shuddering at the touch of her delicate fingers on his arm. "It's just that I'm not all I appear."

"It doesn't trouble me that you're not a rich man, Cope. I don't care that you were poor as a boy, or that you've led a cavalier existence. It's only the present that concerns me. And for that all I need or want is you."

Reid wanted to say the same thing, that if she was truly welcoming him into her family, he eagerly accepted. He wished to flatter and entice her, meld their disparate lives into a single union. But somewhere, south of the Arkansas, loomed a shadow that kept him silent. Fortunately, Boone led his brothers over at that moment, and while Aurelia assigned tasks to her barefooted, shirtless, soggy-haired sons, Reid began slicing a loaf of wheat bread.

It wasn't until after lunch that the real fun began. Edith Ann and Patience collected pewter plates and cups while Aurelia returned scraps of food to her baskets. Reid was about to offer his help when six arms reached out. Captured by surprise, Reid was dragged halfway to the river before he managed to shake Jordy one way, Charlie the other, and wriggled loose of Boone's unsteady grip.

"He's stronger than we thought," Boone observed.

Charlie nodded his agreement, then turned away. It proved a mistake as Reid pounced on the thirteen-year-old, slung him over one shoulder, then deposited him, flailing arms and screeching voice, in the river.

Jordy raced over and jumped atop Reid's back, and a soggy Charlie soon joined him. Reid wrestled both to the ground, locked them in vise-like grips, and awaited Boone's charge.

"Boone, help!" Jordy whined.

"Boone!" Charlie shouted.

But Boone preferred to leave his brothers on their own, and Reid pinned them, then mercilessly tickled the both of them. Edith Ann and Patience, to make matters worse, cheered Reid on, and even Aurelia gave a wild hurrah. Reid then relented, and the boys scrambled to their feet, both of them wearing a considerable quantity of sand and grit, together with smiles about a foot and a half wide.

"Truce?" a breathless Charlie asked, extending his arm.

Reid gripped the elder boy's hand, then took Jordy's as

well. The weary boys rested their heads against Reid's elbows, and he instinctively drew them close a moment before stepping back.

"You're a good wrestler," Charlie observed. "For an old man."

Reid started to retaliate, but the youngsters raced off toward the river, leaving their would-be attacker to himself.

"I could use a hand putting the food away," Aurelia called, and Reid hurried to her aid. As they repacked the back of the wagon, she gripped his arm. Her fingers trembled.

"Aurelia?" Reid asked.

"I thank you for that," she whispered. "Hunt used to wrestle with them, take them hunting, teach them things."

"They seem to have learned what's important. You taught them."

"Not everything. You showed Charlie how to shave."

"Boone would have."

"Cope, I haven't welcomed many men into my world. With the hotel and four children, my life has been awfully full. Just now, though, I feel a rare need."

"I know about needs," he told her. "But we've only just gotten acquainted."

"Have we?" she asked. "I feel like I've known you forever."

You don't know me even now, Reid wanted to tell her. But he couldn't form the words on his lips. Then he realized Boone had left.

"Why, yes, an old friend happened by," Aurelia explained.

"Oh?" Reid asked."Who was that?"

"Lucinda Whitaker," Aurelia replied. "I suppose you probably met her at the tavern. Her father owns the establishment, and Lucy works there. Boone and Lucy have grown up together, though they seldom see each other anymore. I can't imagine how she found us out here."

It wasn't by accident, Reid thought.

They completed packing the wagon. Then, while Aurelia inspected the girls' needlework, Reid excused himself and set off across the sandy hills and wicked ravines in search of Boone Henley.

It wasn't hard to track Boone down. He and Lucy had left a clear trail, the kind a child could follow. Approaching unseen was another matter altogether. It required using a circular route, then easing forward along the wall of a shallow ravine. By slowly, quietly edging ever closer, Reid managed at last to behold the worried faces of Cle Smith and Holland Sisk.

"Haven't you found us a way yet?" Sisk cried. "Boone, you said somethin' 'bout costumes."

"The actors don't get here till next week," Boone explained. "I'm doing my best. I have to work, you know."

"Doin' a lot o' that today?" Smith asked.

"This was Mama's notion. You think I could run off and not be noticed? Sheriff Donley asked me some questions the other day. He's been around more than usual."

"Boone, you wouldn't back out of our agreement, would you?" Smith asked.

The look in the young outlaw's eyes worried Reid, and he instinctively felt around for his rifle. It wasn't there. All he had was the pocket Colt, and it lacked the range to challenge the pistols bobbing on the hips of the outlaws.

"Boone, you know my life's in your hands," Sisk pointed out. "I've never let you down, have I? We've got money. You're welcome to a share. That way you can go to your eastern college and be a lawyer."

"I'd never touch your money," Boone told them. "How would I explain it to Mama? I'll do what I can because you asked me. Only remember this, Hollie. There are lots of people around hunting that reward. It isn't safe for us to meet like this, out in the open."

"Lucy's watchin' the road, remember?" Sisk asked.

"There are lots of roads," Boone argued. "I'll do what I can."

"Know you will," Sisk said, resting his hands on Boone's

shoulders. "You've always been my friend, Boone. Don't let me down."

"I won't," Boone promised.

Smith and Sisk escaped out the far end of the ravine, and a grim Boone Henley turned toward the river. Reid pursued the outlaws a hundred yards before they mounted horses and rode off toward the south.

I almost had them, Reid thought, slapping his thigh. He then made a wide swing south and east, then returned to the wagon.

"Where did you disappear to?" Aurelia asked.

"Had a personal duty to attend to," he told her. "Is it time to leave?"

"No, not unless you wish to. The boys are having a fine time racing each other across the river, and Boone's yet to come back."

"I'm back!" the seventeen-year-old called from behind the wagon. "Was just checking the harness."

"Why don't you go have a look at your brothers?" Aurelia suggested.

"Actually, I hoped to talk to Mr. Reid a minute," Boone explained.

"I think Mr. Reid might enjoy sitting awhile, Boone," Aurelia answered.

"No, I'm all right," Reid told them both. "Why don't we walk down and spy on your brothers a bit, Boone? We can talk along the way."

"Sure," Boone readily agreed.

Reid gave Aurelia a shrug of his shoulders, then started toward the Arkansas. Boone followed closely.

"I'm in trouble, Mr. Reid," Boone whispered once they passed from his mother's view.

"Oh?" Reid asked. "Does this concern Lucy?"

"No, sir," Boone said, laughing. "It's not that sort of a problem. Lucy's just, well, the messenger."

"I'm not certain I understand."

"That's for the best," Boone declared. "I wouldn't want you to wind up where I am."

"Where's that?"

"In the middle. See, the thing is, I've got these friends. You know. We talked about them before. They've managed to get their faces on some wanted posters. They're holed up, Mr. Reid. Every time they try to leave the state, somebody spots them."

"What did they do, Boone?"

"Stole some money. Or rather helped somebody who did. I asked them to give up the money, to let me speak to Sheriff Donley for them."

"And they refused, didn't they?" Reid asked.

"Yes, sir."

"And still they want you to help them escape?"

"They're my friends. I feel for . . . well, one of them's like a brother. He lost his folks early, Mr. Reid. Nobody ever gave him much of a chance, and most people were ready to set their dog on him. He went bad, I'll admit, but it wasn't altogether his doing."

"He's keeping the money, though, isn't he? Must be a considerable amount."

"I don't know," Boone declared. "I wouldn't touch a dime of it. I'd turn it all in, you know, if I knew how. I don't stand with stealing, but it's not for me to say. I only know I want to help keep friends of mine from getting killed. You understand how I feel. You lost friends in the war, didn't you?"

"That was different," Reid argued.

"Sure, but dead's dead. You've traveled a lot, Mr. Reid. Is there a way to get them south, to Mexico maybe? Can it be done?"

"Might be," Reid admitted. "Be risky. Ride south through the Nations and along into Texas. Not the easiest trail."

"Better than walking up a gallows."

"They don't hang boys for stealing," Reid pointed out. "At least not that I've heard of. Is that all they've done, son?"

"All I know. Posters say dead or alive, though, and I've heard talk of hanging."

"You know a man who helps could be in for a hard time himself," Reid warned."My advice would be to tell them to set off south, down the Western cattle trail. Leave them to whatever happens."

"They'll expect more of me."

"Ought to be satisfied you didn't hand them over to Donley," Reid argued. "You know, Boone, you can't carry other folks' burdens the rest of your life."

"Maybe not. But I have to do something."

"I pray you don't wind up being the one to pay the price, Boone. That's often how it ends."

"Maybe so, sir. Maybe so."

They watched Charlie and Jordy swim for another half hour. Then Aurelia called that it was time to conclude the picnic, and Boone headed down to the bank to hurry his brothers out of the river. In half an hour Reid was sitting in the wagon bed with the boys, listening to Patience Framm share an old Norwegian folk tale.

Following a bath and dinner, Copley Reid applied the first strokes to a family portrait he planned for the Henleys. It was to be a surprise—a farewell gift of sorts. He could tell from Boone's wrinkled brow that Smith and Sisk wouldn't be patient much longer. Soon things would come to a head!

Even so, the painting seemed to cast other concerns off into some half-forgotten valley a universe away. As he worked on the background, it seemed eerie how meaningless a picture was until the figures appeared. So long as Aurelia, Edith Ann, Boone, and the boys were mere swirls of pale pigment, the canvas remained worthless.

Copley Reid couldn't help wondering if the same wasn't true of his life.

His thoughts were interrupted by a hurried knock on the door. Reid set his brush aside, then walked to the door and opened it.

"Mr. Reid," a confused Jordan Henley spoke, "Sheriff Donley sent me up here with a message for you."

"Sheriff Donley?" Reid asked, taking a small envelope from the boy's fingers.

"Said it was important, too," Jordy added. "You in trouble?"

"No, of course not," Reid declared, removing his painting frock and grabbing his hat. "I'll attend to it at once."

"Aren't you going to read the note?" the boy asked.

"Oh, yes," Reid said, tearing the corner of the envelope, then peeking inside. He'd already recognized Garner McFarlane's initials on the envelope. Inside was the railroadman's calling card. On the back was scrawled "Jail."

"Can I see?" Jordy asked.

"Not this time," Reid answered, locking his door, then hurrying downstairs. Jordy followed, spraying a dozen questions. Reid left them and the boy behind, though, as he exited the Chester and hurried to the jailhouse.

"You can appreciate our concern at the lack of progress," McFarlane explained as they sat together in Donley's office. "I expected you to have those culprits in hand by now."

"If it makes you feel better, I've got a fair idea where they are," Reid explained. "Saw them both this afternoon, but I didn't have a clear shot."

"Oh?"

"People were in the way. I'm close. Trust me to settle the matter to your satisfaction."

"There's a considerable amount of money at stake, Reid."

"And my life!" Reid barked. "Before you send word to me like this again, you should know I take a dim view of anybody putting me in peril. Do it again, mister, and I'll walk away from this business faster than you can stomp your foot."

"I only intended . . ."

"I don't care," Reid said, slamming a hand down on Donley's desk. The sheriff trotted to the door, peered inside, saw that no harm was being done, and returned to his nephew's desk.

"It's time you settled with those two," McFarlane said, taking his hat and starting for the door.

"Maybe so," Reid agreed, blocking the door. "That's for me to decide, though. You, McFarlane, have a simpler job. You stay right here for an hour, then leave by the back door."

"I'll do nothing of the kind!"

"Then you find Sisk and Smith yourself," Reid said angrily.

"I'll remain as you suggest," McFarlane relented.

Suggest? Reid asked himself as he left the office and slipped out the side door of the jailhouse. It had been a long time since Copley Reid had made suggestions, especially to fools like McFarlane. Who did he think he was dealing with?

And yet as Reid returned to the hotel, he realized the railroader was correct about one thing. It *was* time.

But time for what? Reid asked himself. Time to leave? Time to settle accounts? Which one?

CHAPTER 15

COPLEY Reid found escape in a sound sleep. He awoke the next morning before the sun cracked the eastern horizon. There was something about the stillness that possessed Esmeralda at that predawn hour that set his mind at rest and sharpened his thinking. He hurriedly dressed, taking great care to slip the pocket pistol inside his vest. He then grabbed his leather rifle case and set off down the dim staircase toward the darkened streets.

He wasted no time reaching Abner Ryder's livery. Ryder himself was fast asleep, but Reid located a straw-haired boy of perhaps twelve asleep in an empty stall.

"Sir?" the boy asked warily when Reid's boot stirred him to life.

"I need a horse," Reid announced.

"Kind o' early to go ridin'," the youngster observed. "Mr. Ryder don't . . ."

"You leave Ryder to me," Reid instructed as he tossed the boy half a dollar. "Saddle the bay for me, and be quick on your feet."

"It's still dark out there."

"I'm well acquainted with the dark," Reid explained as the boy lit a candle and scrambled into a pair of overalls. "I find a brisk ride gets my blood pumping."

"Just the same, you watch the gopher holes," the stableboy warned. "They're particular bad down by the river. Just last . . ."

"Thanks for the warning," Reid said, motioning the boy to hurry his work. "I know my business."

"Guess you do," the youngster said, staring a moment at the bulge in Reid's vest. "Won't be long, sir."

The boy was true to his word, and the bay stood saddled and ready for the ride in a matter of moments. Reid dropped the required silver dollars in Ryder's hire box, then nudged the horse into a light trot. By the time the far horizon glowed amber, Copley Reid was splashing through the shallows of the Arkansas, bound southward.

There hadn't been so many riders crossing southwestern Kansas that Reid had difficulty locating the trail of the two outlaws. Even in the faint light their tracks, together with those of a third horse, likely belonging to the girl from the tavern, were clear to see. They headed south and a bit west from the ravine where Smith and Sisk had met with Boone Henley.

"Fools!" Reid muttered as he followed the tracks down a well-traveled road. Wtih grassy hills and numerous rocky creeks all around, it would have been a simple thing to hide one's tracks. Instead the young criminals were making it easy. Too easy, Reid worried. He kept a sharp eye out for trouble, and his ears listened for any sound which didn't belong. In the end, though, nothing out of the ordinary attracted his attention. The one horse split off on the trail to Peabody's, and the other two continued along until they approached a dugout farmhouse.

"So, here we are at last," Reid whispered as he concealed his horse in a copse of trees. He then opened the rifle case and assembled the Alsweig. He carefully slipped a single deadly bullet into the firing chamber and closed the bolt. There remained nothing but the waiting. Soon the hunt would be over, concluded by a pair of whining projectiles.

As he lay on the dewy slope, cradling the rifle and studying the farm, Reid wondered what it would feel like when that conical sliver of lead tore into the outlaws. Oh, he'd seen men die. Some screamed and others gasped in disbelief. But as to the sensation, well, there was no telling. Would it come like long-denied rest, or would death explode in a fury of pain and convulsion?

It will only come, Reid told himself. What does it matter to you? Yes, they're young, and maybe they didn't have the smoothest trail to walk, but they chose to ride with the Stapletons. Now they will die.

There was a cold inevitability to the morning. Even as the minutes passed, and no one inside the dugout stirred, Reid never doubted what was sure to transpire. Perhaps Sisk would limp to the well to draw water, and Smith would step to the woodpile. They would go about their chores as any young men. Only when a shrill whine punctuated the dull whacks of his ax would Smith turn his head. Even then he wouldn't notice Holland Sisk lying face down in the grass beside the well. Only when the second bullet slammed into his own chest would Smith realize what was happening. But then it would be too late. He would be dead.

No other ending was possible, Reid told himself over and over. But as the sun climbed ever higher, doubts began to haunt him. His fingers began to cramp, and he tired of the wait. Would Smith and Sisk sleep the day away?

"Have a long night, did you, boys?" Reid whispered. "Visit the tavern?"

No, they had come directly to the dugout. Tracks didn't lie. Could they have left? No, it just wasn't possible. Where would they go?

Reid swallowed deeply, set the rifle aside a moment, and checked his pistol. It was a new Colt, finely balanced. It felt oddly comfortable in his hand. He'd given the bullets a lighter charge to avoid the tendency of pistol bullets to tumble downward away from a man's vitals. It generally took two such light bullets to kill a man certain and fast. But a man with a shooter's eye could place his shots as he chose, and Reid favored hitting a man over filling a room with smoke and noise.

Of course, the pistol wasn't much use from beyond fifty

feet, but close in, it could kill well enough. Reid frowned at the thought. He had grown weary of the game. He rose to his feet, cocked the hammer, and started slowly, cautiously toward the dugout.

It was maybe a hundred yards to the makeshift sod and plank cabin. Reid approached slowly. With each step, Reid grew increasingly anxious. He sniffed smoke in the air, but not a puff exited the chimney. Except for a rattling shutter and a singing cardinal, not a sound left the dugout. Arriving at the door, Reid took a deep breath, then jumped inside, pistol at the ready. A can stirred on the right, and Reid fired, sending a prowling raccoon fleeing for its life. Then, blinking his eyes in disbelief, Reid beheld the deserted dwelling.

"So, you've found another lair, have you?" Reid asked, lowering his gun. At his feet lay piles of discarded clothing, empty tins, and chicken bones. There was a foul, confined smell to the place, and he hurried outside.

I should have had the rifle yesterday, Reid chastised himself. It would have been easy to drop them both at the ravine. Boone was close, though, and Aurelia would have seen it all. How would she look upon him then?

It didn't matter, Reid decided. She would know in the end anyway. A hunter couldn't hide behind sketchpads and canvases forever.

Reid located tracks leading from a nearby shed out into the hills. Tracking two riders cross-country wasn't nearly as simple a task as following a clear trail along an established road. There was but one refuge in that particular direction, though—Peabody's tavern. So Reid repacked the Alsweig, mounted his horse, and headed for the saloon.

Peabody's place was not frequented by early risers. As it happened, when Reid arrived, he found the tavern deserted save for a pair of buckskin-clad men sleeping off a drunk in one corner and a pleasant-looking young woman who was sweeping the floor.

"Good morning," she said, gazing warily at Reid.

"Hello, Lucy," he said, recalling the name Boone had used. "I suppose it's a bit early for refreshment."

"I can sell you whiskey or apple cider," she answered with a stiff lip. "If you want, I can even fry up some eggs and a few slices of bacon."

"That would be just fine," Reid said, taking a seat at a table facing the door. "Cook breakfast for anybody else this morning?"

"Just my family," she said, setting the broom aside.

"Nobody else? Maybe a couple of youngsters, close to your age, one with a strong limp?"

"I don't know who you could be talkin' about," she answered.

"It's against the law, aiding outlaws," Reid told her. "There's a reward, you know."

"You got proof I done anything wrong, you tell the sheriff," she said as she drew a side of bacon from the larder. "As for rewards, you'll discover not everyone sells out his friends for a few greenback dollars."

"You could help them, Lucy," Reid argued. "If they keep running, somebody's bound to put a bullet in them."

"Oh?" she asked. "I hear the man does that wears spectacles and uses a fancy rifle. Know anybody like that?"

Reid felt her icy gaze tear through him. He hadn't imagined anyone would know him to be on the trail. But, of course, Smith and Sisk would recall the whine of the Alsweig, would alert their spies. Had they told Boone as well? Had the boys been doing the spying?

Reid kept silent that next half hour. He ate the breakfast Lucy prepared and sipped a cup of hard cider that burned his throat and left his eyes watering. The food and drink seemed to settle his nerves, and he set out from the tavern resolved to locate the quarry.

Smith and Sisk left few clues, though, and Reid rode mile after mile across creeks and ravines, over hills and through tall grasses. He ached from hours in the saddle, and when he neared the small railhead town of Sherlock, he welcomed the chance to dismount.

"Well, sir, I saw a couple o' riders like these two a bit ago," the depot clerk admitted when Reid showed him the poster. They ain't been back. If they happen by, you can count on me droppin' 'em, though. That reward'll come in handy with my Jane abed with her fifth on the way."

"Anybody come through trying to buy a ticket west the last few days?" Reid asked. "Young girl maybe?"

"West?" the clerk asked, scratching his ear. "No strangers headed that way. Not this week."

"Well, you watch out for any," Reid advised.

"Think those two'll come here?"

"It's the closest station," Reid explained. "A man in a hurry to leave Kansas is bound to try the fastest route."

"Well, well," the clerk said, grinning. "Reward surely would come in handy. Yes, sir, with all those dollars I can . . ."

"Sure," Reid said, excusing himself. "You hear or see anything, wire McFarlane."

"Surely will," the clerk promised.

Reid left Sherlock in defeat. He had no hint as to where the outlaws might be hiding. There were posters about, but now that the outlaws were alerted, they would be difficult to locate. It was no doubt the handiwork of that Lucy Whitaker! Or, he thought glumly, of Boone Henley.

That thought plagued Reid as he rode back toward Esmeralda. It was near nightfall when he returned to Ryder's livery, and both horse and rider were exhausted.

"Been a day of it, huh?" the stableboy asked as he took charge of the weary bay. "She's done in."

"See she gets something extra in her feed bag," Reid said, tossing the boy a shiny silver dollar.

"Honey and oats," the boy announced. "And a lick o' sugar, too."

Reid watched with satisfaction as the stableboy unsaddled the tired animal and led it to a stall. Once saddle and bridle were put away, the boy lovingly provided feed and water before taking out a brush.

"You got a name, son?" Reid asked as he sat atop the stall.

"Most people do," the boy answered. "Mine's Andy, Andy Cooling."

"Work here long, Andy?" Reid asked.

"On and off a year and a half, Mr. Reid."

"You know me?"

"Well, Mr. Ryder was some curious as to who had the bay, and when I described you, he came to your name quick enough."

"Tell me, Andy, you've got a way of noticing things, don't you?"

"Pa always told me only a fool keeps his eyes shut."

"Maybe you could take a look at a picture I've got here in my pocket. I'm looking for these fellows, and . . ."

Andy climbed atop the stall and snatched the poster. Then he hopped back down so that he could hold the poster closer to a nearby lantern.

"I've seen 'em," Andy muttered.

"They're wanted men, son."

"Yeah, I've seen posters before, Mr. Reid. You know the one of 'em's Cle Smith, Mr. Ryder's nephew."

"Thought as much."

"I don't know that he'd have me spreadin' tales about his family."

"Well, don't speak of him, then," Reid advised. "Tell me about the other one. Seen him lately?"

"Might have," Andy admitted.

"I've been known to be generous to my friends," Reid pointed out. "You may have noticed that already."

"Yes, sir," Andy agreed, turning the silver dollar over in his fingers. "These the ones you were lookin' for today?"

Reid nodded, and the boy laughed.

"See them?" Reid asked.

"Yes, sir, I think I did. That's somethin', ain't it? You went lookin' for them, and they rode right into Esmeralda while you was gone."

"Where were they?" Reid asked, climbing down from the stall. "Where did you see them? Who were they with?"

"They were alone," Andy explained, growing a little nervous at Reid's sudden impatience. "At the Alhambra Saloon. I took their horses in around noon. They picked 'em up later on, while Charlie Henley was mindin' the place."

"Which way did they go?"

"South, toward the river," Andy explained. "But I heard 'em talkin' 'bout makin' camp along the river."

"You're a wonder, Andy," Reid said, smiling broadly as he gripped the youngster's shoulders and handed over another silver dollar.

"You a federal marshal, Mr. Reid?"

"No, railroad detective of sorts," Reid explained.

"If you catch 'em, think maybe I might be in for some o' the reward?"

"Maybe," Reid answered. "Especially if you keep all this to yourself. Don't tell anybody."

"Not even Ma?"

"No one," Reid insisted. "Keep your eyes open. If you see anything, send me word at the Chester."

"I will, Mr. Reid. I promise."

"Watch out for yourself, Andy. Those two have friends hereabouts."

"I can take care o' myself," the boy declared. "We'll catch 'em next time they ride in here for sure."

Reid nodded, then headed for the stable door. Soon he was striding down the street toward the Chester, the scent strong in his nostrils.

They must be nervous, coming to town like that, Reid thought. Nervous? No, desperate was a better word for it. It was only luck that had kept them from dying that day. A man couldn't rely on that kind of blind luck twice, though. Next time the Alsweig would do its work, and the business would be concluded.

Reid promised himself that.

CHAPTER 16

COPLEY Reid made his way up the steps and along inside the Chester Hotel. He'd grown to feel almost at home in the large lobby, with its fine maple chairs and colorful carpets. And yet he felt different that evening. Something was odd, out of place. Perhaps it was carrying the leather case with its deadly contents that caused Reid to be self-conscious as he approached the desk. Or maybe it was because for the first time in days he'd missed sitting at the dinner table with the Henleys. He wasn't sure about the reason, but the change was unmistakable.

Reid wasn't the only one to note the change, either. When he reached the front desk, young Charlie Henley pulled out the key and passed it to Reid with an odd hesitance.

"Mama missed you being at supper," the boy mentioned. "Andy down at the livery said you took the bay out."

"Felt like a ride," Reid explained. "I didn't sleep too well last night."

"Mama'd gone along."

"Didn't want to trouble her. I left early."

"I know. Jordy went to fetch you to breakfast, but you'd gone already. Andy said you took your pistol, too."

"Precaution," Reid answered nervously. "Never can tell what you'll come upon riding unknown country. I shot a snake once riding the Arkansas."

"Sure," the youngster said, the suspicion lingering in his eyes.

"Guess Boone must be feeling poorly," Reid said, shifting the subject. "I never knew you to man the desk in the evening."

"I'm getting older," Charlie boasted. "Not much to do this time of night anyway. As for Boone, he had some visitors."

"Old friends?"

"I think so," Charlie said, growing cautious. "He had a message this morning. I haven't seen him since breakfast."

"Oh?" Reid asked. "He's been gone all day? With no word? He could be in trouble. Maybe somebody ought to have a look."

"No, he's fine," Charlie said, brightening some as he read Reid's concern. "Jordy and I saw him over at the Alhambra around two o'clock. Later on he dropped by the livery."

"But he wasn't at dinner?"

"Don't go worrying," Charlie said, grinning. "I saw him make up a food basket in the kitchen. I think he took a girl down to the river."

"Figure he's having a private picnic, huh?"

"Guess so," Charlie said, laughing.

Reid shared a grin, then took his key and turned toward the stairs. He got less than halfway when Aurelia intercepted him.

"Where have you been all day?" she asked, blocking his path. "Oh, dear, plainly on horseback. I'm afraid you brought back a trifle much of the horse with you."

"That's likely so," Reid admitted. "I was a bit more in the saddle than I intended."

"You didn't ride off alone?"

"Yes, ma'am, I confess I did."

"That's not so wise a thing to do, Cope," she complained. "Kermit Donley's had men riding the river in search of outlaws this past month. Next time do ask me to go along. Or take Boone. It's best to have a guide along."

"This morning I needed the solitude," he argued.

"You don't need to get killed," she responded.

"Little chance of that," he said, touching the pistol on his hip. "I can protect myself."

"Oh, you wouldn't even know what to be afraid of," she scolded. "I'll wager you've eaten nothing all day, too."

"I had a fine breakfast at Peabody's."

"That awful place!" she exclaimed. "Now come along. I'll heat you up some stew myself. I fear the pie's all gone. Jordan ate the last half by himself, the little scoundrel. But there's bread left."

"Then I'm certain to be satisfied," he said, following her along past the dining room, then slipping into the kitchen as she held wide the door.

It was rather pleasant, sitting at a small table, watching Aurelia Henley cook. She didn't seem the type to put her hands to ordinary tasks, and yet she was at home at the stove. Aurelia was, after all, a fraud. But then who was Copley Reid to think such a thing?

The stew was delicious, and he ate liberally. The ride had given him an appetite, and he twice emptied his bowl. All the while Aurelia spoke of the theatre company due next week from Philadelphia.

"We were to have a troupe here this week, but they canceled at the last minute," she grumbled. "The Philadelphia company does Shakespeare, you know. We're to have Richard III and Hamlet this year."

"Not the lightest of entertainments," Reid observed.

"Well, I suppose some might prefer comedy, but with four children, I find myself rather more amused than I care most days."

"And life is serious."

"Yes, it is," she agreed. "You haven't done much painting since you completed my portrait. Don't you have a commission to complete?"

"Yes," he said, frowning.

"How far along is the work?"

"I suppose you could say I have the preliminary sketches complete," he told her. "Now comes the hard work."

"I would have thought the planning was most difficult."

"Not always," he said, steadying his hands. "Sometimes it's the final few brush strokes that prove the greatest challenge."

"Yes, I can see how they would be," she agreed.

"And now I think I'll excuse myself and see if I can wash the horse off me," Reid said, rising from the table.

"Tell Charlie to have hot water sent up," she suggested. "And if you decide to go riding again tomorrow, send me word. I'll ride along."

"Thanks, but I suspect I'll feel like the horse rode me come daybreak. Thank you for the late supper. It was wonderful, and I fear to have starved without it."

"Just the house's way of seeing its guests well-tended," she said, smiling brightly.

"I know better than that," he replied. "Thank you, Aurelia."

Reid then turned and left the kitchen. After telling Charlie about the bath, the weary man climbed the stairs to his room, put his leather rifle case in its secure place behind his valise, set aside his pistol, kicked off his boots, and awaited the arrival of the bath water.

Charlie and Jordy brought the water a quarter hour later, and Copley Reid lay in the bath until the water grew tepid. Even then, his stiff muscles only reluctantly allowed him to leave the tub. As he fought to rub life back into joints, he cursed Smith and Sisk for leaving the dugout, for roaming the countryside and proving such elusive prey so near the end of the chase.

Reid took to his bed rather early. He sat in his nightshirt, sketching in the faint glow of an oil lamp as the wind gently rustled the curtains. Anyone else might have thought it a quiet, peaceful eve. Copley Reid saw events sure to come, though, and he found no solace in his vision.

Reid did manage to lose himself in his painting. He'd sketched Edith Ann at the piano, then added Aurelia, smiling proudly from behind her daughter's shoulder. Boone,

Charlie, and little Jordy now completed the picture, their uneven voices joined in song.

"It will make a fine portrait for the ballroom," Reid told himself. "A fitting farewell gift."

Around nine o'clock a knock on his door interrupted his labor.

"Yes?" he called.

"It's me, Charlie, Mr. Reid," the caller declared. "Can I come inside a moment?"

"Likely another message from McFarlane," Reid muttered as he set aside his brushes and welcomed the boy inside. Charlie carried no envelopes, though. Instead he cautiously made his way inside, sat at the foot of the bed, and stared nervously out the window.

"Something worrying you, son?" Reid asked.

"I'm not sure," Charlie explained. "Shouldn't, I know. It's just, well, I never knew Boone to keep secrets."

"Secrets? What sort of secrets?"

"I told you he took some food tonight. Mr. Reid, he didn't tell Mama. She got mad at the cooks for it being missing. Isn't like Boone to get anybody in trouble. He's not back, either. I'm worrying some."

"Don't," Reid said, tossing the bedding aside so that he could sit beside the boy. "I know where he's gone, Charlie. He's just helping some friends. He's sure to be back soon."

"He told you?"

"In a way, yes," Reid explained. "I'll talk to him about the food, tell him he should explain to your mama so the cooks won't be blamed. Will that make you feel better?"

"Sure will," Charlie said. "Strange how things work out. When you came in wearing that pistol tonight I was half thinking you were some sort of paid killer."

"What put such a thought in your head?" Reid asked.

"Jordy said the sheriff sent for you last night," Charlie explained. "And, well, you don't seem to do a lot of painting. Sorry I was suspicious."

"No need," Reid said, walking over to the wardrobe and slipping into a pair of trousers. "A boy with no papa ought to look hard at visitors. It's wise not to size anybody up too fast."

"That's what Boone always says."

"Well, he's right again. Now why don't you run along? I'll bet you're about due for bed. Didn't get any singing done tonight, did you?"

"No, Mama thought it best to give Edith Ann a rest. She worked awful hard this morning making up for the picnic yesterday. And Boone's gone, too."

"He'll be along," Reid assured Charlie.

The boy sprang to his feet and hurried into the sitting room. He paused long enough to dip buckets into the tub, fill them with cool water, and empty them out the window. Once the tub was empty, he took the buckets along with him and left Reid alone in the room.

It was sometimes amazing how a thirteen-year-old could so quickly set aside his concerns. Well, Reid might have answered Charlie's questions, but others remained. What was keeping Boone out so late?

Reid knew that answer. More troubling questions followed.

Would Boone return at all, or had he left with his friends?

Reid suspected young Henley would come back, but there was no certainty to anything. That had been proven often enough.

"How deep a hole are you digging for yourself, Boone?" Reid whispered to the window. Loyalty was a fine thing, but no friend was worth hanging for. Or taking a bullet.

Reid waited close to two hours before finally detecting a single slender shadow threading its way around the side of the hotel. Even in the dim light, Boone Henley's bony shoulders and slight frame stood out. Reid slipped on a shirt, then stepped into his boots and began the slow, quiet walk to the small room shared by the three Henley boys on the second floor. The light leaking from beneath the door told of

Boone's arrival. Reid knocked lightly, then waited for an answer.

None came for several moments. Then, finally, the door moved, and a pale Boone Henley, blue nightshirt dangling over his bony legs, greeted Reid's questioning eyes.

"Mr. Reid?" the young man cried, sighing with relief. "I thought it was Mama. Lord, I confess I'm relieved."

"Why's that?"

"I was out pretty late," the young man explained. "She didn't send you, did she?"

"No, I came of my own accord," Reid explained.

"And why's that?"

"Guess you're entitled to that question," Reid admitted. "Not often you get such a late caller."

"No, sir," Boone agreed. "Is there something the matter?"

Reid glanced inside the room. Charlie and Jordy appeared to be dozing peacefully. But appearances, as Reid knew only too well, could be deceiving.

"Why don't we step down the hall to the library for a few moments?" Reid suggested.

"Just let me get my robe," Boone said, walking softly to the wardrobe, draping the robe around him, then returning to the door. The two of them then walked to the library. Once inside, Reid lit a lamp, then pointed toward a pair of adjacent chairs. They seated themselves.

"You asked if something is the matter," Reid began. "It is."

"Sir?"

"Ever see either of these fellows?" Reid asked, passing the wrinkled wanted poster into Boone's trembling hands.

"I might have," Boone said, tapping his fingers on the table. "I see a lot of people across the desk."

"These posters are all over town, Boone. And I doubt you would have met these two as hotel guests. They're outlaws. They rode with the Stapleton brothers."

"Yeah, I've seen the posters," Boone confessed.

"You knew them before, though, didn't you?" Reid added,

passing into Boone's hand the yellowing photograph of the three youngsters in front of the Chester.

"Where'd you come by this?" Boone cried.

"In an abandoned camp well east of here. It wasn't far from where Tom Stapleton's body lay."

"I don't understand."

"I know that, Boone. Part of you doesn't want to understand, either. These boys were friends of yours once."

"They still are."

"You don't even know them now. They've robbed and lied and maybe killed, Boone. They'd do all three—to you, if that meant holding onto the money they've accumulated."

"You don't know how it was for them," Boone said, dropping his face into his hands. "Holland never played anybody false. His father beat him half to death when he was six. By the time he was twelve, he was off on his own. A farmer near killed him at fourteen."

"For what, Boone? As I understand it, the boy was entertaining the man's wife. And what about young Smith? He stole half his uncle's stock. Maybe they had a rough hand to play. Well, others have, too. You lost a father, but you didn't rob a bank or shoot a stage driver. I understand the kind of obligation you feel for these friends, but they just aren't worth the price you'll have to pay."

"And what's that?"

"Prison at best. Maybe worse."

"Prison?" Boone cried. "For what?"

"Aiding their escape. Hiding them."

"I haven't . . ."

"Boone, I saw you with them at the river the day of the picnic. I followed their tracks to that farm. Where did you take the food tonight? The river?"

"Lord, who are you?"

"You know my name, Boone."

"Then tell me what you are."

"Just now I guess you'd call me a detective of sorts. Or maybe a tracker."

"You're the one Hollie says is hunting him, aren't you? The one with the rifle?"

"I'm the one that will shoot them if it comes to that."

"If it comes to that?" Boone said, shaking his head violently. "I don't believe any of this! You're supposed to be my friend. I expected you to help."

"I plan to, Boone. I'm going to help you get those friends of yours in to Sheriff Donley, maybe even get them an amnesty from the railroad."

"What?"

"The A, T, & S F doesn't want them, Boone. All they want is the money the Stapletons got away with. Your young friends have that money. If they'll turn it in, I'm certain any charges can be done away with."

"You want me to turn Hollie and Cle over to the sheriff?" Boone asked. "You lied to me. What makes you think I'd ever trust you now?"

"You have to, Boone."

"Why?"

"Because I'm the only one who can help you."

"Help me? How? By betraying my friends?"

"Boone, you only owe honor to honorable men. These two are thieves."

"You don't know them. Cle only held the horses. He never even went inside any of the places."

"And Sisk?" Reid asked.

"He found out things, got information."

"He doesn't wear that pistol for decoration, Boone. Any way you figure it, I can get the charges dropped if you'll get me the stolen money. Whether they did or didn't help steal it, they're holding it now."

"There's a lot, isn't there?"

"Better than fifteen thousand dollars, I'd guess," Reid explained. "Boone, if I wanted to go that route, I could have gone to Sheriff Donley, gathered some men, and trailed you to them tonight. You might have gotten hurt that way, though, and I don't want that. It's best this way. It's bound to end soon, one way or the other. My way those friends of yours walk away."

"And if they won't give up the money?"

"Then I'll gather it up after they're dead," Reid said coldly. "I will, too, Boone. You tell them that."

"You ask a lot. They won't be too happy to hear me tell them you've followed me."

"No, they won't," Reid said, frowning. "You know them best, Boone. If you think it's dangerous, maybe you should stay here."

"They're my friends," Boone argued. "I have to try."

CHAPTER 17

HOLLAND Sisk and Cle Smith had spent a restless night huddled beside a small fire on a horseshoe-shaped sandbar in the Arkansas River. It was the worst kind of place, open to wind and plagued by mosquitoes. But at least the approaches lay open to view. They were both well-acquainted with the work done by the high-powered Austrian rifle, and neither desired the swift, whining death brought by the little man with the spectacles.

"We should've gone back to the Mitchell place," Smith grumbled as he fought to work the kinks from his back. "Hollie, we can't stay out here. We stick out like sheep in a cow pasture, and somebody's bound to happen along and spot us."

"That'd be their poor luck," Sisk declared.

"No, it'll be ours," Smith argued. "Shots'd bring company, and besides, it might be a pair o' schoolboys or else some woman. Couldn't shoot them."

"Guess not," Sisk admitted. "At least not now. But I'm gettin' around to that point, Cle. I feel like they're closin' in on us. We best get shed o' this country soon or plan on bein' buried here."

"I'll take some killin'," Smith boasted. " 'Less I starve. Any food left from that sack Boone brought out?"

"Not a crumb. We should've rationed it, I guess. Lucy's due out this mornin', though. She'll bring bacon and some biscuit."

"If she gets away from her pa. Hollie, maybe we ought to just ride south and take our chances."

"Maybe," Sisk said, frowning as he gazed toward the wilds

south of the river. "Be long odds our gettin' away, though. I'd rather wait on Boone figurin' somethin'."

"I'll wait the balance o' the week," Smith declared. "Then I'm for leavin'."

Sisk nodded his agreement. Yes, it was time to do something. Sitting around only worsened the odds. Bounty men sniffed around in search of a scent, and those posters weren't going away.

Their attention was suddenly seized by the sound of a horse splashing into the shallows downstream. Sisk pulled a pistol and dove for the scant cover provided by his saddle. Smith swung a rifle in the direction of the visitor and calmly waited. A bounty man might have been greeted with a hail of gunfire. Lucy Whitaker found a friendlier welcome.

"Bring us some breakfast?" Smith asked, setting aside his rifle.

"Bacon and biscuits," Lucy announced, grinning at Sisk. "And news as well."

"First the food," Sisk said, holstering his pistol. "I'm nigh starved."

"I never knew a time when you weren't," Lucy remarked as she climbed down from the saddle and handed Cle Smith her horse's reins. "For one thing or another," she added with a grin.

Sisk embraced her warmly, then spread out the contents of a provision bag on his blanket and began meting out portions.

"I won't be able to come down here again, I fear," Lucy whispered as her companions devoured the food.

"Why not?" Sisk asked through a mouthful of biscuit.

"Papa's grown suspicious," she explained. "And there's that other man, too."

"What man?" Smith asked. The color drained out of the young outlaw's face, and he drew his rifle close.

"A stranger," Lucy explained. "He rode over yesterday from the direction of the farm. He looked to have been riding hard, Hollie. He asked questions, and he watched me a good bit."

"What'd he look like?" Sisk cried.

"Was he a little man, with spectacles?" Smith added.

"He was," she answered.

"Lord, I knew he'd be around in time," Smith said, gazing wildly around at the distant plain.

"He's the one who's been chasin' us, Lucy," Sisk elaborated. "He's the very devil, a bounty killer who works for the railroad. Shot Newt Franklin and the Stapletons, and he wants us, too."

"Hollie, this wasn't the first time that little man's been to Peabody's," Lucy said nervously.

"What?" Sisk asked.

"He came before," she said, frowning.

"Oh?" Sisk queried, seeing there was more to tell.

"Boone brought him out," she added.

"Lord, that can't be!" Sisk shouted. "Not Boone! It's just not possible he could help a bounty man."

"Maybe he was just leadin' him down a false trail," Smith suggested. "That could be it. Sheriff hangs around the Chester, you know."

"They seemed mighty friendly," Lucy went on to say. "What's more, I saw the little man down at the river the day you met Boone. I'm not sayin' they've done business, Hollie. Just that I'd be careful how far I'd trust Boone."

"We're careful with everybody," Sisk insisted. "But Boone? We were countin' on his help."

"Well, we've seen little enough of it," Smith grumbled. "Still, he could've turned us in yesterday when we were in town, and he didn't."

"Maybe he wants the reward all to himself," Lucy said. "Maybe he worried he could get hurt."

"I won't believe it," Sisk argued. "I offered him money, a lot more'n the railroad'd pay out in reward. Boone and me, we're like brothers. You don't sell your blood for greenbacks, Lucy."

"I only know what I see," she countered. "All I got to say is be careful. Don't trust him too far."

"Thanks for the warnin', and especially for the food," Smith said, stepping over to where he'd tethered Lucy's horse.

"I don't think I'd stay here much longer," she advised as she mounted the horse and prepared to return to the tavern.

"If we don't get by the tavern before leavin', Luce, know that I'll send for you once I get settled," Sisk promised.

"Sure, you will, Hollie," she said, her smile growing faint. "Don't you always?"

"I got money this time," Sisk reminded her.

"Wasn't money we ever needed," she said sadly. "You watch your hide, Holland Sisk. Write me sometime."

Before he could make another pledge, she kicked her horse into a gallop and set off through the river toward the tavern.

"You ought to send for her, all right," Smith said as they watched her dust trail settle. "She's better'n most women I've come across."

"Wouldn't be a favor," Sisk argued. "She wants a settled life, and me, I'm for excitement."

"You may get a fair share 'fore we clear Kansas," Smith remarked. "Lord, who'd thought Boone to throw in with a bounty man?"

"We don't know he has!" Sisk barked. "I won't hear it said. Understand, Cle?"

"I understand just fine, Hollie. Boone said we could disguise ourselves, go with those theatre folk. Well, what happened to that plan? We got to find a different direction to travel now Boone's suspect. What'll we do?"

"Best chance lies goin' west," Sisk pointed out. "Sherlock's the closest depot."

"They spotted us there once," Smith reminded his cohort.

"May do it again, too. Still, it's the best choice."

"Then I say we best get ridin'," Smith said, kicking sand over the ashes of the fire. "I'll fetch the horses."

"I'll get the cash," Sisk replied.

In his months riding with the Stapletons, Holland Sisk had learned to take precautions, especially where money was concerned. Frank Stapleton had taught him the trick of burying the cash box, but it had been Holland's own notion to bury it beneath the campfire. A layer of rocks insulated the money from any heat, and the charred ground concealed signs of digging. Holland easily swept aside the sand and ashes with a small spade, then uncovered the box. He opened it long enough to gaze with wonder at the thick piles of banknotes.

"Makes even the runnin' sweet, doesn't it?" Smith called.

"Be even sweeter spendin' it," Sisk replied as he closed the box and carried it along toward the saddles. The cash was best concealed in the center of a blanket roll, then tied behind a saddle. As Sisk attended to that chore, Smith fixed bridles and saddle blankets.

"Be best to take precautions with that stationmaster," Smith suggested as Sisk heaved his saddle atop his horse. "He spotted us straight off last time."

"No, we'll want to swing northeast of Sherlock Station," Sisk pointed out. "No need botherin' the folks at the depot. We'll come in on the cars from the blind side."

"Freight cars, you mean?"

"With luck, we can sit atop a load of plows and wagon wheels all the way to Pueblo."

"And if some guard spots us, that'll be his bad luck," Smith declared with a cruel grin. "No posters'll be waitin' for us in the Rockies."

"Up north to the Union Pacific, then along to California!"

"No more little men with big rifles!"

"Just freedom. How will it feel, bein' rich, Cle?"

"Like a dream," Smith answered. "Nobody'll talk about runts or lame legs then."

"There'll be girls aplenty, Cle. We'll buy ourselves the finest of everything!"

"Everything!" Smith echoed.

With minds filled with wondrous dreams of a better future, the two outlaws mounted their horses and crossed the river. Soon enough they would be aboard a westbound freight headed for better times, safe from bounty men and posters, leaving behind dark days and nightmare memories.

They reached Sherlock in the middle of the morning. It wasn't much of a town, just a huddle of buildings at a railhead surrounded by scattered farms and ranches. Holland Sisk couldn't help remembering a similar station at Banwell Junction. Banwell, too, had appeared near deserted, what with the population already toiling in field or pasture. And if not for that rifle in the loft . . .

The two riders swung north from the Arkansas, taking care to keep from view. The railroad tracks were empty.

"No cars on the sidin'," Smith grumbled. "Not much cover, Hollie. Maybe we'd be better off ridin' down, buyin' tickets."

"No, I recall the schedule well enough. Westbound usually pulls in before midday," Sisk said as he dismounted and tied his horse to a small cottonwood. "Be better to make a try toward dark, but this way we're not apt to find any surprises."

"Me, I've had enough o' them," Smith declared.

They waited close to two hours for the westbound freight. It pulled up slowly, with a hint of hesitation. While fuel and water were taken on, a team of freight handlers slid open the side door of a boxcar and began unloading goods.

"We'll leave the horses here," Sisk announced as he slung his blanket roll over one shoulder. "Let's try for the last car, Cle. Doesn't appear to be anybody watchin'."

"No," Smith agreed, wrapping his own blanket around a rifle. "Lot o' open ground 'tween here and there, Hollie."

"I know," Sisk admitted. "Wish I had a better notion, Cle. Got any ideas?"

"Come on," Smith said, leading the way.

They got to within twenty yards of the train before anyone took notice. A boy working the water pipe called out, and a railroad guard appeared beside the caboose.

"Hollie?" Smith asked nervously.

"No need to panic," Sisk whispered. Instead he waved at the guard and continued on.

"Where you boys headed?" the guard called.

"Thought to catch a ride on this train," Sisk replied. "Been down on our luck o' late. No ranch work to be found, so we thought to . . ."

"Keep those hands in view, mister!" the guard barked. "Got a bad limp, don't you? Didn't happen to pay a call on Newton Station a couple o' months back, did you? I picked up a bullet in my leg that day. Hey, Baker!"

The moment the guard turned his eyes toward the train, Cle Smith discarded his blanket and shot the guard through the neck. The guard spoke hoarsely, then clutched his throat and fell.

"Let's get clear o' this place," Sisk urged as he turned toward the cottonwoods a hundred yards away.

"Go along, Hollie," Smith urged, crouching in the grass and firing at the train. "I'll cover you a bit."

"Cle?"

"Get along!" Smith shouted, and Sisk limped onward.

For ten minutes Smith exchanged fire with a pair of railroaders. None of the bullets found a victim, for Smith wasn't aiming at anyone in particular, and the railroadmen, having seen one of their number fall, chose not to risk exposure and a like fate.

But once word of the outlaws' appearance spread to the depot, the character of the fight changed. A pair of bounty men, attracted by reward dollars, mounted their horses and set off in pursuit. The two of them rode furiously toward the escaping outlaws, and had not Holland Sisk been already mounted, the end of the Stapleton gang might well have been made at Sherlock that very morning. As it happened, Holland led Smith's horse toward the station, and Smith climbed atop the animal even as the bounty men charged.

"Not today," Smith declared as he fired his rifle. Sisk opened up with his pistol as well, and the bounty men returned fire. In all, twenty bullets must have split the Kansas morning. A horse makes a poor shooting stand, though, and amid the smoke and confusion no projectile found its mark. One of Smith's rifle bullets did cripple the lead bounty rider's horse, though.

"Time to ride," Sisk announced as the horse went down.

"Ride?" Smith asked. "Where?"

"Follow me," Sisk urged, starting eastward. The remaining bounty man shouted a challenge and raced after. Smith steadied his mount, then took aim and waited. When the pursurer was only fifty yards distant, Cle Smith killed his second man. The bounty man's head snapped back as if snared by a rope, and he rolled off the saddle like a discarded flour sack.

"That's one won't do any more chasin'," Smith boasted. "And that guard might be done for, too."

"Yes," Sisk agreed as he slapped his horse into a gallop.

They spoke no more of it until crossing the Arkansas.

"They'll think twice 'fore they come after us now," Smith declared. "Now they know there'll be a price paid."

"Now they'll shoot on sight," Sisk muttered. "And those posters'll say murder, Cle."

"They already say 'dead or alive,' " Smith reminded his friend. "This makes no real difference at all."

It will to Boone, Holland Sisk knew. And to others. He cursed his misfortune, then turned his horse toward Peabody's tavern and the last hope of refuge he could imagine. Lucy would help. Maybe she would know some way . . .

Holland Sisk and Cle Smith appeared at Peabody's, dust-covered and fearful. Their wild eyes revealed panic and desperation. They found no welcome, either. Lucy stared fearfully out of a side window. Her father, shotgun in hand, barred the door.

"You ain't welcome here, boys!" Whitaker shouted.

"Mr. Whitaker, we only came to pick up some supplies," Sisk argued. "We just need . . ."

"You need to get to ridin'!" Whitaker yelled. "Or else get filled with buckshot. Don't you think I know you're posted? There've been men by here a dozen times lookin' for you. I could pick up some dollars droppin' you both, but I'm mindful o' Lucy's feeling's."

"Please, Mr. Whitaker," Sisk begged.

"I told you to get!" Whitaker barked. "You ain't welcome here, Holland, and neither are your intentions! I've raised a good girl, and I don't aim to see her trifled with more'n she's been already!"

"You're a hard man to send those in need away," Smith argued.

"Hard?" Whitaker asked. "You boys ain't dead. Consider yourselves lucky."

"Hollie, I could shoot that old man," Smith said, turning to his friend.

"Or him you," Sisk answered. "Is that what we're gettin' to be, Cle? Killers? Let's go."

Smith frowned heavily, then turned and followed Sisk northward. There was but one hope left—Esmeralda.

They swung well east of town, though. Sisk knew how eagerly Old Man Whitaker would set a posse onto their trail. It wouldn't do to ride into a town full of waiting riflemen. Or even one.

"Horses won't stand this kind o' rough handlin'," Smith warned after a time.

"There's a farm nearby," Sisk said, pointing to a thin line of white-gray smoke across the hillside. "Kendall place. We'll swap our mounts, get some food."

"Now there's a fine idea," Smith agreed.

And although Louis Kendall was a bit alarmed by the appearance of unexpected company, especially the kind that smelled of powder smoke and cold sweat, he wasn't about to lose an opportunity to profit by their misfortunes. He swapped out horses willingly enough, especially when Sisk threw in two hundred dollars, and Alice Kendall provided a generous supper for another twenty-five.

"What manner o' trouble you boys come across?" Kendall asked as he helped tie provision bags behind his visitors' saddles.

"Never you mind yourself with that," Sisk warned. "If a man knew too much, he might get himself shot."

"Oh, I'm as ignorant as sin," Kendall proclaimed. "Don't know a whit!"

"Best keep it that way," Smith warned.

The two fugitives then set out once more. A chill wind seemed to blow them north toward the river, then west toward town.

"You don't mean to take us to Esmeralda, do you?" Smith cried.

"Can't count on Lucy now," Sisk explained. "Dugout's likely crawlin' with bounty men. As for the river, well, they wouldn't neglect lookin' there, would they? Your uncle might help."

"Might help shoot us, you mean," Smith grumbled.

"And there's Boone."

"He'll help," Smith declared.

"Sure he will," Sisk said, wiping his forehead.

"Yeah, he'll help," Smith vowed. "He'll help, or else he'll regret the day he was born!"

CHAPTER 18

LIKE the spider who had carefully spun his web, Copley Reid awaited events. To the south, bounty men searched the plain, eager to collect the railroad reward. Stationmasters along the Atchison, Topeka, and Santa Fe line kept a sharp watch, cutting off escape via rail. Elsewhere lawmen like Kermit Donley scoured the countryside, looking for the criminals. The net was dropping on Sisk and Smith. And now, with Boone Henley torn by doubt, their last hope of aid was fast slipping away.

"Now you must be desperate indeed," Reid mumbled as he read the short telegram from Sherlock. Fools! Did they imagine they could board a freight car in broad daylight and attract no attention? A man with a limp like Sisk!

The telegram carried darker tidings as well. A raid guard was dead, as was a bounty rider. Another was hurt. That bade ill for Sisk and Smith. A day before they had been renegade boys, doomed to prison perhaps. Now a hangman's rope awaited their capture.

Boone Henley would find the news bitter indeed. The young man would have a choice to make, and hard feelings were sure to rise from the choosing. Reid pondered the dangers that choice entailed for Boone, for Aurelia, for Copley Reid. Would any of them truly survive the consequences?

Reid devoted the afternoon and most of the evening to watching Boone's every movement. The young man couldn't help noticing his new shadow. Boone's once-steady hand wavered as he marked the ledgers, and his voice betrayed anxiety. He was short with his sister and brothers. At dinner, he even barked at Aurelia.

"I think it best you excuse yourself from the table," she told Boone. "When you regain your civility, we'll welcome your return."

Boone stalked off down the hall. Moments later Reid excused himself and followed.

It was Reid's intention to draw the boy aside then and there, but Boone holed up in the laundry, and Reid decided to walk Front Street a bit. He managed to confer with Andy Cooling and a pair of town boys paid to watch stables and back roads.

"Nothin' yet, Mr. Reid," Andy relayed. "I heard they kilt a man in Sherlock. Likely they gone west."

No, they would come to Esmeralda. Reid knew it.

"I'll let you know if I see 'em," Andy promised, and Reid returned to the hotel.

He located Boone in the library. The boy was staring at the picture on the wall, concentrating hardest on the faces of two Shoshoni boys huddling beside a campfire.

"I'm partial to those boys myself," Reid announced as he sat at the table.

"That's how it was for Holland and me," Boone explained. "We were always together, sharing the worst winter could hand us. We only wanted to move along, get away."

"It's hard losing friends," Reid observed.

"I haven't lost anybody yet," Boone said, slamming his hand down on the table. "Mr. Reid, you said you were the only one who could help. What exactly did you mean?"

Boone's probing eyes seemed to bore right into Reid's heart. The hunter turned self-consciously away, but Boone hurried over and sat beside him.

"You said you could help!" the young man cried.

"Up until this afternoon I hoped I could work out some sort of deal with the railroad," Reid explained sourly. "After all, there wasn't anybody pressing a murder charge. Oh, there was plenty of proof they rode with Frank Stapleton, but the law can be forgiving of the young. Real issue was the money."

"If it was returned, Hollie and Cle could go free, couldn't they?"

"All that's changed now," Reid said, soberly eyeing Boone. "They tried to board a train today at Sherlock."

"They're not dead?" Boone asked, shuddering.

"They're not," Reid muttered. "They tried to climb aboard a freight car, but a guard spotted them."

"And?"

"That guard's dead now, Boone. Another fellow, too. Nothing on earth can save those boys from here on."

"It couldn't have been them!"

"Why?" Reid asked. "Because they swore they'd lay low, camp down by the river and let you figure things? They've got fifteen, twenty thousand dollars, Boone. Think about it. Money like that breeds impatience."

"I don't believe you," Boone said, turning away.

"Here," Reid countered, tossing the telegram onto the bare table. "Read for yourself."

Boone started to rise, then halted. Instead he took the telegram and read it carefully.

"What's it mean, 'resolve this matter'?" Boone asked.

"Bring it to an end," Reid explained. "It means hunt them down and shoot them. What do you think it means, Boone? What else is there to do?"

"You can't," Boone argued, swallowing hard. "They're my friends. You are . . . were, too. You could help them get to Mexico. You could . . ."

"Son, it's over," Reid insisted. "You tried to help, but they've crossed the line."

"What?"

"There's a line civilized folks draw, Boone. It says these are the things you can do, and these others you can't. A man crosses that line, he's got no place among good people anymore. I guess you'd call him a renegade, a rogue, somebody to track down and get rid of."

"I don't believe any of this."

"People have to have laws."

"Maybe they do! But it seems to me the same law that would hang Hollie for shooting a man trying to kill him allows others to ride out and shoot a man down without even so much as a hail. What sort of law is that?"

"The kind we live with," Reid answered. "You wouldn't hold it against a man who shot a prowling wolf, would you, Boone?"

"Guess not."

"The men I've shot are no better than wolves. Worse, I'd say. Wolves don't prey on their own kind."

"I just can't believe you can be the same man who painted my mama's portrait! How could anybody who can turn a bit of oil paste into magic hunt men down and kill them?"

"It isn't the same man at all," Reid replied. "Maybe one day you'll understand how a man can put his better side away and let the darker part of his character take charge. I can't begin to explain it. But there's no need, Boone, because it's not me that matters just now. It's you."

"Me?" Boone cried.

"Yes, you. There are two things you have to know tonight, Boone Henley. One is that those boys you called friend a few hours past are now desperate. They'll have no place to turn save you. The second thing is that if they'd altogether trusted you to help out, they never would have ridden to Sherlock and tried to get aboard that freight."

"It would be crazy to come into town," Boone argued. "People know them. I know a dozen who have been out looking for them, trying to collect that reward."

"They'll come, Boone," Reid insisted. "They won't ask, either. They've crossed the line now, son, and they won't mind shooting again. You better figure out what you'll do and say."

"They won't come."

"They will, Boone," Reid said, turning the seventeen-year-old's face so that their eyes met. "You know I'm right. I'll be close. And ready. You send word when you spot them and leave me to handle things."

"Kill them, you mean."

"It's bound to happen, Boone. I'll make it short and painless. Hanging's a pitiful hard way to die."

"No!" Boone shouted, racing away from the table and down the hall.

"Yes," Reid whispered to the silent room. He then stumbled through the door and climbed the stairs to his room. The Alsweig wanted cleaning. There were plans to make. Lord, why was it the hard things always fell on the young?

"You know I'm right!"

The words rang through Boone Henley's ears as he hurried down the hall toward the small room he shared with his brothers. Right? How could he be? It wasn't in Holland's nature to hurt anybody. Holland Sisk knew pain. He would never, could never inflict hurt on anyone else.

Boone didn't want to believe otherwise. And yet the words continued to hammer at him. They rang through his mind with a fatal truth. And yet there was no ignoring the old bond forged in a hundred boyhood trials.

Boone rummaged through his chest until he located the yellowing photograph retrieved only recently from Copley Reid. Those three boys seemed so young. There was a hint of waywardness to their smiles perhaps, but what fourteen-year-old didn't seem caught by imagination and wanderlust? It wasn't hard to understand how Hollie and Cle could be caught up in depot robberies. Was that so different from swiping Grandma Hoover's pies or raiding old man Mitchell's melon patch?

But murder? Boone closed his eyes and tried to see it. He envisioned a railroad guard swinging a rifle toward Holland's head. But nothing, no touch of terror or madness, would bring Holland to shoot another human. He hadn't even struck back when the knife had severed his hamstring. If ever a man had cause . . .

There was Cle Smith, though. Poor, maltreated Cle. Something dark rested behind Cle's eyes. A world of swallowed pain sometimes welled up in Cle until it threatened to explode. If prodded to desperation, Cle could kill. Perhaps that was how it had happened. If so, Holland was again trapped by fate and circumstance.

As I am, Boone thought.

He remained alone, staring at the photograph, for close to an hour. Finally Jordan hopped over and sat beside Boone on the edge of the bed.

"You weren't much bigger than Charlie then," the younger boy remarked. "That's Holland there, isn't it?"

"Yeah," Boone said, sighing.

"Figure they'll catch him, Boone? I heard Andy say a couple of posses are out searching the river."

"I hope not," Boone mumbled.

"They shot some people in Sherlock, you know."

"I heard that, Jordy. They're my friends, though."

"Yeah," Jordy said, sighing. The twelve-year-old then rolled off the bed and began working on his school lessons. Charlie appeared shortly, glanced at Boone, then took out a book and began reading.

On toward nine o'clock their mother arrived to listen to prayers and bid them good night. She paused a moment with each of the younger boys, then drew Boone out into the hall.

"Boone, you're not in trouble, are you?" she asked.

"No, Mama," the young man insisted.

"Kermit Donley said Holland Sisk and the Smith boy were spotted at the river this evening. They killed a couple of men this afternoon. One had a wife and six children. They wouldn't come here, would they?"

"Mama, it would be crazy," Boone told her.

"I know you have strong ties to Holland, Boone, but you can't allow yourself to make the kind of mistake he did. You would pay for it the rest of your life."

"I won't, Mama."

"Promise me?"

"I . . . promise," Boone said, clasping her hands. Once her shoulder had provided solace and consolation. But when she pulled him closer, he stepped away. He was no longer a child to need a midnight lullaby or a whispered reassurance. He was seventeen, as near a man as he ever would be.

"Look after your brothers," Aurelia Henley said for the thousandth time as she turned to leave. Boone nodded, then slipped inside his room and bolted the door. Charlie and Jordy had already climbed into their beds, so Boone undressed, slipped a nightshirt over his bony shoulders, and put out the lamp.

No rest came, though. For seemingly hours Boone stared at the swirling darkness all around him. Every creak of a floorboard seemed to warn of approaching danger.

They won't come, Boone told himself again and again. But Reid's words overwhelmed him: "You know I'm right."

Somehow in spite of his tortured soul Boone Henley managed to fall asleep. He dreamed of arriving at a great eastern university, surrounded by a pack of admiring strangers. Fame and fortune were certain to follow Boone Henley. Everyone knew that. Just as he was about to embrace an emerald-eyed beauty, a small hand roused him.

"Wake up, Boone," Jordy whispered.

"What?" Boone cried, forcing his eyes open. "Go back to sleep, little brother."

"Boone, you better wake up," Jordy said, trembling. As Boone's eyes sharpened their focus, they detected the fear in the smaller boy's eyes.

"Boone?" Charlie called from the far side of the room.

Boone jumped out of bed and stared in disbelief at the ugly steel barrel of a pistol resting beside Charlie's ear.

Holland Sisk held that gun. Cle Smith stood in the doorway, cradling a Winchester rifle.

"Hollie?" Boone cried. "Cle?"

"Won't you welcome us in?" Holland asked. "You'd have us think ourselves unwelcome."

"You're not," Boone said, waving his old friends into the room. "But you've no call to point guns at my brother."

Charlie scrambled away and sought the imagined safety of Boone's side. Jordy huddled in the far corner.

"We wouldn't've come here, but there was no place else," Cle explained, bolting the door. "Boone, we need help."

"I don't have much to offer," Boone told them. "Not after Sherlock."

"That wasn't our doin'," Cle began. "Was that fool guard. He challenged us, and he fired first."

"And the other one?"

"Was a bounty man," Holland explained. "You know the kind. Riffraff out of the Indian Nations, I'd guess. He won't be missed."

"The guard had a wife," Boone told them. "Six kids, too."

"That's hard news," Holland said, lowering his pistol and dropping his chin to his chest. "I was hopin' he'd pull through anyway. He would have shot us, though, Boone. You got to believe that."

"Does it matter? Hollie, Cle, the whole countryside's full of people looking for you. And right upstairs, or maybe down the hall, watching you come in here, is the very fellow you've been running from."

"Oh?" Holland asked.

"Copley Reid. A smallish man with spectacles. He's been looking for you."

"He's the one that shot the Stapletons," Cle mumbled. "He won't get us that easy."

"He will if he's really out there," Holland grumbled. "Any way out of here 'cept the hall, Boone?"

"Just out the window and straight down," Boone explained.

"That's no good," Holland declared. "There's a deputy watchin' the front door, and another across the street. Side one's all that's not guarded."

"It leads from the kitchen," Charlie said nervously. "It's locked up till breakfast."

"How do we get there?" Cle asked.

"Walk right down the hall, take the stairs, and you're there," Boone replied. "Unless that Reid fellow's out in the hall with a rifle."

"If he is, we'll settle this once and for all," Cle boasted.

"Hold on, Cle," Boone pleaded as Smith reached for the bolt. "You can't start shooting with my brothers in here."

"If we let 'em leave, they're like as not to warn somebody," Cle argued.

"Wait, Cle," Holland objected as Cle again reached for the door bolt. "Boone's right to urge caution. We need to make a plan."

"We wait for mornin', we'll be dead, Hollie."

"Boone, you got a notion what we might do?" Holland asked.

"Give up," Boone said. "If you turn back the money, the railroad might . . ."

"Give back the money?" Holland asked, laughing. "Boone, you gone crazy? I've near been shot twice to keep this money. It goes where I go. And I plan to get clear o' this town."

"I can't help you," Boone said, shaking his head sadly.

"Oh, you can, Boone," Holland said, turning the pistol toward Charlie once more. "You can, and you will."

"Don't do this, Hollie," Boone pleaded. "I'd help if I knew a way, but . . ."

"There has to be a way," Cle argued. "Sheriff's partial to your mama, as I recall. He's not likely to start any shooting if she's with us."

"No!" Boone cried, rushing toward the two friends who seemed instantly to have turned into monsters.

Holland jabbed the pistol's barrel into Boone's gut, and a sharp pain doubled Boone up and dropped him to the floor.

"Boone?" Jordy cried, scrambling over beside his brother. "You hurt him, and I swear . . ."

"Shut up!" Cle barked. "Charlie, come along with me. Let's see if we can rouse your mama. Hollie, you look after these two."

"Done," Sisk answered. "You ought to know better than to draw against a pat hand, Boone. Now you just sit there nice and quiet while we sort this mess out."

Boone fought off a wave of nausea and hugged himself. A rib ached. Likely it was broken. That was the least of his worries, though. Jordy rocked fretfully on one side, and Holland stood on the other, cocked Colt ready to deal death. And in the adjacent room Cle had Charlie, possibly Edith Ann, and . . . even their mother.

"You know I'm right," Reid had said.

I do now, Boone admitted. But now it was too late.

CHAPTER 19

COPLEY Reid lay atop his bed, dozing lightly. He hadn't bothered to undress. He anticipated trouble before morning, and there would be no seconds to waste. When a knock on the door finally roused him just after dawn, he sprang instantly to his feet and hurried into the sitting room, grabbing his pistol in the process.

When he opened the door, he gazed down at young Andy Cooling. The stableboy's eyes were red from lack of sleep, and he yawned before announcing his news.

"They're here," Andy whispered. "Cleophus and the other one. They left their horses down the street and came up the back way."

"They're inside the hotel?" Reid asked.

"Second floor," Andy explained. "I followed 'em myself."

"You'll get yourself killed taking chances," Reid said, frowning. "You get along to the jailhouse, find Sheriff Donley."

"You goin' after 'em?"

Reid nodded soberly, and Andy grinned.

"Can't I stay?" the boy pleaded. "I never seen a real shoot-up."

"Pray you never do," Reid said sourly. "Now get along to the jailhouse. Hurry. There's no time to waste."

Andy muttered to himself, then quietly slipped down the stairs as Reid stuffed his pistol in his belt and followed him down.

He'd hoped to catch the outlaws unawares, in the open, not in a crowded hotel room with Boone and perhaps the younger Henleys in the line of fire. Copley Reid preferred the cold, dispassionate death brought from long range, not the hot, frenzied murder done at close quarters, with random chance likely to turn the game sour at any moment.

He hoped perhaps Sisk and Smith might have already left. After all, Boone might turn them away. Or maybe he would even convince his friends to lay down their arms. Reid had little confidence that either would occur. Still, there was a chance of catching the fugitives by surprise, of preventing the bloodshed he so fervently feared.

He started up the hallway slowly, cautiously. The oil lamps had been extinguished, and only a faint gray light entered from the single window at the far end of the hall. The sun wasn't yet high in the morning sky, after all, and someone had lowered the shades. Then suddenly a door swung open, and a solitary figure moved across the light.

Reid instantly pulled his pistol and hugged the wall. The door of an adjacent room opened with a crash, and voices called in alarm.

Reid rushed forward, then ducked behind a linen cupboard. The far end of the hall was full of figures. Only when the shutter was raised could he recognize any of them, though. Charlie and Jordy Henley, their faces pale as their nightshirts, cowered near the door of their room. Boone was equally shaken, though he had taken the time to pull on a pair of trousers. On either side of Boone stood Sisk and Smith, the one waving a pistol and the other holding a rifle. The gun barrels pointed at a stunned Aurelia Henley.

"Boone, what's going on here?" she demanded to know. "What madness is this, breaking in my door?"

"Sorry, ma'am," Sisk said, frowning grimly. "We need your help."

"Holland?" Aurelia cried. "Holland Sisk?"

"Yes, ma'am," Sisk said, nodding.

"You'll hardly find me in the mood to help vandals," she declared. "What do you mean, coming into my home, dragging my sons from their beds, pointing guns?"

"We mean to get out of Esmeralda and hopefully clear of Kansas," Smith explained. "I figure maybe you can work all that out with the sheriff, Miz Henley."

"Boone?" she called, searching her son's face for some explanation.

"It's not that easy," Reid announced, stepping cautiously out from behind the cupboard. "Even if you got clear of Esmeralda, there are men waiting at the river, at the depot, everywhere. Give it up."

"Well," Smith said, grinning. "You weren't lyin', were you, Boone? He's here as you say. Well, I can settle one thing before leavin' town."

"No!" Boone growled, pushing aside the barrel of Smith's Winchester. "You shoot that gun, and the whole town'll be down on us."

"Us?" Aurelia asked. "On them, you mean."

"No, Mama," Boone said, trembling as he turned to face her. "We're right in the middle of this, Jordy, Charlie, me, and you."

"Thank God Edith Ann's already gone to the kitchen," Aurelia said, turning toward Reid as if he might be able to end the nightmare. "Cope?"

"There's no escape," Reid argued. "Sheriff's got men posted. He's likely on his way right this minute. You boys were spotted coming in."

"The devil we were!" Sisk shouted.

"You were expected, you see," Reid explained. "And you walked right into as neat a trap as any ever laid."

"That right, Mr. Bounty Man?" Smith howled, firing a rifle shot at the cupboard. Reid dove to the floor, but the discharge brought cries from the nearby rooms, and a flurry of activity downstairs.

"Fool!" Reid yelled.

"You better figure us a way out o' this!" Smith shouted. "Elsewise I start killin' people!"

Aurelia screamed, and Jordy shrieked as Smith grabbed him by the ear and slung him out into the hall.

"No!" Boone pleaded again.

A door across the hall from Reid opened, and a slender Kansas City cattle broker stepped out to see what was amiss. Smith cranked the lever on his rifle, fired, and the broker fell backward into his room. Reid made a move forward, but Sisk fired past Jordy's helpless form, splintering the wall. Reid dared not return fire, so he withdrew to safety.

"We'll kill the whole bunch," Smith warned. "Hey, Bounty Man, you hear me? I shoot Jordy first, then Charlie."

"Don't be stupid!" Reid replied. "We'll get you horses, take them around behind the kitchen. It's not being watched. But you've got to let the Henleys go."

"No, they're old friends," Sisk declared. "I'll feel a good deal safer with 'em close."

"Boone, how does that set with you, son?" Reid called.

"None too good," Boone said, stepping over toward Charlie, then helping Jordy rise from the floor. "These two are little, Holland, Cle. They won't offer you a shield. Let them go. I'll walk with you instead."

"He's right, Cle," Sisk said.

Boone didn't wait for Smith to consider the matter, just pushed his brothers down the hall, and the two youngsters scrambled past Boone and along to Reid before anyone realized what had happened.

"Smart, Boone," Sisk growled as Reid drew the younger Henleys to cover.

"Only now we'll have to take your mother along," Smith explained.

"Take me!" Boone pleaded.

"No, Boone, you go down to the livery and find us a couple o' good horses," Sisk directed. "Good runners, hear? Meanwhile we'll head on down to the kitchen with your mama, get somethin' to eat maybe. Hear me, Bounty Man?"

"I hear!" Reid shouted in reply."You just make sure you

don't harm her. You do, and there's not a place under the sun you can hide from me."

"Yeah? Well, that's another thing, mister," Sisk added. "We see so much as a whisker of you on that street, we kill her. And Boone, too. Anybody else we can."

"I'll stay right here," Reid pledged. "You won't have any trouble."

"Good. Get the horses, Boone," Sisk demanded. "And keep this hall clear!"

Boone gazed helplessly at Reid, who nodded. The young man then hurried down the hall. Reid shouted for the hotel guests to close their doors and stay clear. Then he dragged Jordy and Charlie along to the library, pushed them in, stepped inside, and bolted the door behind.

Even as the two outlaws' heavy boots thudded down the hall, Jordy and Charlie fought to reach their mother.

"You didn't see their eyes!" Charlie complained. "They'll shoot her."

"No, they won't," Reid promised. "They had it all their way this morning. No longer. It's not their game anymore. Now, it's mine."

Reid spoke with a sort of grim certainty that quieted the boys' fears. As the boots descended the stairs, Reid unbolted the door and stepped back into the hall. Boone stood there, seemingly frozen in his tracks.

"What do I do?" Boone asked. "They've got Mama. Sheriff Donley . . ."

"Will do as he's told," Reid announced. "Go down to Ryder's, saddle a pair of good horses, and lead them around to the back door, the one behind the kitchen."

"And then?"

"Wait," Reid instructed. "Don't worry about your mama. I'll be watching all the while."

"You're going to kill them? They're . . ."

"They're what? Friends?" Reid challenged. "No, they're

strangers now, Boone. Killers. And there's just one thing left for them."

"You don't understand," Boone objected.

"Oh, I understand just fine," Reid assured the young man. "What's more, I know what's to be done. Get along to the livery. Leave the rest to me."

Boone hesitated a moment, but Reid nodded somberly and turned the boy toward the stairs. As Boone descended, Reid began the climb to the third floor. He did, indeed, understand what remained to be done.

Copley Reid reached his room in short order. Then with a measured coolness he opened his leather rifle case and began assembling the Alsweig rifle. There, in his hands, lay the only tool he ever truly understood. With the rifle in his hands, he was the master craftsman. And as he screwed each piece to the next, he grinned coldly. There, in his hands, rested the means to end a nightmare. That precision rifle with the telescopic sight had never failed to find its one target. Sudden, whining death had come to Esmeralda that morning.

As for the shot, everything was wrong. The sun was on the wrong quarter, and Reid's window offered a poor angle. There would be no cover, it seemed. The only other perch was the balcony, and beyond that the protruding roof of the kitchen itself.

Copley Reid had no talent for climbing. He had never been comfortable in high places, and the thin ledge along the balcony rail promised only a long drop followed by short and sudden death. Only a fool would risk it. A fool or a desperate man. Copley Reid was near to being the latter.

"Mr. Reid, no!" Charlie called, entering the room as Reid prepared to ease his way out onto the ledge.

"Know another way, Charlie?" Reid asked.

"To do what?" the boy called.

"Here, hold this," Reid said, slipping the rifle down from his shoulder. "When I get out on the ledge, you hand it to me. Understand?"

"You'll fall."

"No, I won't," Reid muttered. "Can't afford to."

And with that said, Reid eased his way over the rail and onto the ledge. He then took the rifle from Charlie's outstretched hands.

"You get your brother to cover," Reid warned, pointing toward a still-shaken Jordy. "We'll talk more later."

"Yes, sir," Charlie mumbled.

Reid knew the boys felt the world unraveling. Well, perhaps it was. He himself had no time to consider such matters. He firmly gripped the ledge, then lowered himself along the outer wall of the hotel so that his feet came to rest on a lattice of sorts just above a thin ledge on the lower floor. Then, whispering a half-remembered prayer, Copley Reid let go his grip and landed hard on the second-floor ledge. Taking a single deep breath, he finally climbed out onto the kitchen roof and took up station above the door. Moments later Boone appeared with two saddled horses.

"Be along soon's I finish this biscuit, Boone," Holland Sisk called from the door. "You ready, Cle?"

"Mama, you all right?" Boone shouted.

"Boone, you leave those horses and go!" Aurelia yelled.

"No, you wait right there, Boone," Sisk commanded. "Wouldn't do to frighten the animals. That sheriff around?"

"He's here!" Donley shouted from Front Street. "You boys have the street so long as Miz Aurelia's left alone. We'll catch you by and by, though."

"Long as it's later," Smith called, laughing. "Later's always better'n sooner."

Reid frowned. The outlaws were a bit too at ease. Likely they had enjoyed a nip or two. He needed them sharp, if a bit nervous. Too reckless, and Aurelia might yet come to harm.

Boone glanced up at the roof only once. The sight of the rifle filled him with a mixture of relief and fear and, yes, guilt. Copley Reid ached for that boy. Boone had choices to make, and none of them would provide any comfort that evening. Friends, even a mother, might die, and the weight rested squarely on Boone Henley as to which it would be.

"We're comin' out!" Sisk finally announced. "Boone, you give those saddles a hard tug. Wouldn't do if the cinches were loose."

Good, Reid thought as Boone did as instructed. It was best Boone had something to occupy himself. Even better, the outlaws were expecting trouble from a different direction.

"All right, Boone," Sisk said, satisfied the horses were properly saddled. "Ready, Cle?"

"Lead on," Smith replied.

The two outlaws stepped out from the kitchen door then. Sisk led the way, and Smith followed. Aurelia shielded them both from an assemblage of deputized citizens and bounty men crowding Front Street.

Reid swung his rifle so that the back of Holland Sisk's skull filled the sight. The limping outlaw babbled away, but Reid wasn't listening. Instead he took a deep breath and squeezed the trigger.

Sisk heard nothing. Perhaps he never even felt the bullet plunge through his brain. The impact threw Sisk forward and knocked Aurelia to the earth. The outlaw managed no sound, just died in a futile sort of silence that seemed a fitting end to a tormented life.

"Boone?" Cle Smith cried as he dropped to one knee and stared around in dismay.

"Well, Cle?" Boone called, flinging his arms helplessly to each side. "What did you expect? I'm not strong like you. Go ahead and shoot!"

As Smith sought a deadlier target, Copley Reid calmly worked the bolt back, replaced the spent cartridge, and readied a second shot. Smith only located the long rifle the second Reid pressed the trigger. The Alsweig whined, and Cle Smith's answering shot exploded harmlessly into the ground. Smith stumbled backward, clutching his chest and coughing desperately as his mouth filled with blood. Then Sheriff Donley and two others fired a short volley that ended Cleophus Smith's pain once and for all.

As the smoke settled earthward and bystanders recaptured their wits, Reid descended the roof and satisfied himself that Boone had Aurelia in hand. Only then did Copley Reid inspect his handiwork.

Boone cradled Holland Sisk's limp head and stared woefully into his mother's reddening eyes.

"I'm sorry, Mama," the young man muttered.

"Aurelia, are you all right?" Lindsey Rankin asked as he helped her up.

Others appeared, and soon a crowd collected around the corpses.

"Would you look at that?" Garner McFarlane said, tearing open the lining of Sisk's coat. "The money's there, all right. Sheriff, help me get the bodies down to the depot, will you?"

"Best check the boots, too," someone suggested. "Must be ten thousand at least there."

"More, I'd bet," another added.

"Well, you said all along you'd tend to it in time," McFarlane said, turning to Reid. "I'll see you get your promised share. Care to witness the count?"

Reid shook his head in disgust, and McFarlane motioned to a pair of bystanders to lift the bodies.

"Guess it makes you feel fine, shootin' those boys down like that," Sheriff Donley said, scowling. "You took a chance, Reid!"

"No, they were dead the minute they stepped outside that door," Reid said sourly.

Donley started to speak again, but Reid turned and stepped around the lawman. He marched around the side of the hotel, passed a stunned Edith Ann, saw Charlie and Jordy race past, then stepped inside the deserted lobby and made his way upstairs. He sat alone in his room, coldly disassembling the Alsweig. Then he opened his vest and tossed the pistol aside.

CHAPTER 20

IT was Boone who first appeared at Copley Reid's door. The seventeen-year-old seemed older than before. His hands and clothes were stained by dried blood, and his eyes were red and swollen.

"Your mama all right?" Reid asked, waving Boone inside.

"Oh, she's stronger than she might seem. Shook some, I'd guess, though she won't show it. She's stronger than you think when you first see her."

"And the boys?"

"Scared, but it's sure to pass. I thank you for getting them clear, Mr. Reid. If they'd been down there, too . . ."

"Sure," Reid said, sitting in the corner chair. Boone remained standing.

"I guess I made a mess of it," the boy finally blurted.

"You did what you could," Reid argued. "A man can only do his best, you know, Boone. Once they shot that guard at Sherlock, there was just one direction left for things to turn. They would have found it hard to turn over all that cash anyway. I'd judge there was maybe twenty-five thousand in all."

"I feel like I failed everybody!" Boone exclaimed. "Mama, Jordy and Charlie, most especially Holland."

"He failed himself," Reid said, rising. He took a step toward Boone, and the young man's face paled. Boone retreated, then came forward in a rush. The boy leaned against Reid's shoulder, perhaps seeking a strength that wasn't there. Charlie appeared at the door with a large square covered by a blanket then, and Boone walked away to the corner.

"What's this?" Reid asked.

"Mama's picture," Charlie explained as he removed the blanket.

"I feel like we forced you to do it," Aurelia said, following the boys into the room. "I don't see how we can keep it now."

"Nobody's forced me to do anything since I was fourteen years old!" Reid countered. "I meant it as a gift. Whatever else, I never go back on a bargain fairly made."

"Fairly?" she asked. "You lied to me. Worse, you've used my son, my hotel, and me! I don't know that I can ever forgive that."

Reid nodded sadly. Perhaps it was inevitable. After all, he'd learned that like the masterpiece that had so long eluded his brushes, love and belonging were rarely achieved and very seldom kept for long.

"I don't know that I'd expect you to feel otherwise," he finally told her. "I never intended a one of you should come to danger, though, and I wish you'd keep the picture. It belongs here, even if I don't."

"Mama?" Boone asked, his eyes inviting acceptance.

"I'll take it back downstairs," Charlie grumbled. "You'll have to help me hang it, Mama. Mama?"

She nodded, then gave a last, sorrowful glance at Copley Reid before leaving the room. Boone lingered a bit longer. Reid knew there was pain there which longed to share itself, but it was a father's ear that was needed, not that of the man who had struck down the friends of youth.

Boone left without speaking another word. Copley Reid then collected his belongings, taking care to leave his sketches of the children and the family portrait in the room. He then carried his valise and the leather gun case down the long flights of stairs.

"Leaving?" Boone asked when Reid placed his key atop the desk.

"It's best," Reid announced. "Tally my bill."

"The painting squared that," Boone explained. "Mr. McFarlane came by. He left a note for you."

Reid took the small envelope and opened it. Inside were a few remarks, a tally of the stolen money, and instructions to stop by the depot office and collect bank drafts for the reward due.

"Where will you go now?" Boone asked as Reid pocketed the note. "England? Austria? Topeka?"

"Anywhere," Reid said, sighing. "It doesn't matter."

"Wherever a rifle's needed, eh?"

"No, I think I'll try the brushes awhile. You brought me back to them, Boone, you and your mama. I'd forgotten that life."

"I wish I had such choices," Boone grumbled.

"You do, son," Reid argued. "There's an eastbound express leaving the station in an hour. A westbound departs after dinner."

"I've got no money," Boone said, shrugging his shoulders.

"Yes, you do," Reid said, drawing out his wallet. He placed first one, then a second hundred-dollar greenback on the desk. "Not enough?" Reid asked. "Stop by the depot. There's more."

"I guess it's not the money after all," Boone said, nudging the bills back toward Reid.

"No, it never is," Reid declared. "It's direction, purpose, that boxes you in. I've been thinking about Colorado lately. No one's ever quite captured the Rockies on canvas. It would mean some traveling, making camp out in the open even. Of course, I'd have to have a secretary, someone I could depend on. Know a man who needs a job?"

"I might," Boone said, trembling slightly.

"He's got a job," Aurelia announced from the lobby. "Besides, there's plenty to paint right here in Esmeralda, remember? This hotel lodges the heartbeat of the country. You haven't even rendered your sketches in oil yet, and . . ."

"There are other considerations," Reid pointed out.

"Yes, I'd guess that to be true enough," Aurelia admitted. "But if you based yourself here in Esmeralda, you could still go elsewhere from time to time as the urge came. You could make your sketches, then return here. I'd keep a room ready and waiting. A suite even, so you'd have your own studio."

"Is that all that would be waiting?" he asked.

"I'd be here," she said, stepping closer. "My heart would be waiting. In time, though, there would be a price."

"Usually is," Reid observed. "A high one?"

"For some men," she answered. "For others, not so much."

"What would it be from me?"

"A ring," she said, taking his hand in her own. "Is it a fair offer?"

"Monumentally satisfactory, madam," Reid said, lifting her hand to his mouth and kissing it. She rested her tired head on his shoulder, and a terrible longing seemed to devour every inch of Copley Reid. He shuddered, then held her close.

"Does a married man still need a secretary?" Boone asked.

"Secretary, and perhaps student," Reid answered.

"And son?" Aurelia whispered.

"Yes, that especially," Reid agreed.

Boone smiled wearily, then gripped Reid's proffered hand. Slowly, gradually, a warmth seemed to flow from mother and son into Copley Reid, displacing the emptiness and chasing away the encroaching fingers of despair.

Why was it, Reid wondered, that he had thought Esmeralda a remarkable name for the place? True, the Kansas plain held an undeniable austerity. But the town, after all, held the rarest gems of all—peace and love. And perhaps, for Copley Reid, belonging.

If you have enjoyed this book and would like to receive details of other Walker Western titles, please write to:

Western Editor
Walker and Company
720 Fifth Avenue
New York, NY 10019